'You're visiting me without your wife?

'Assuming,' Taryn continued, 'that you've tied the knot since you've been away?'

Was it possible Mike had finally stopped carrying a torch for his ex-fiancée, the irresistible Crystal, and married someone else? Or was he still a free man?

He gave a short laugh. 'Marriage isn't high on my list of priorities.'

Taryn felt inexplicably buoyed all of a sudden. Because he hadn't married anyone? Why should that buoy her? He'd be the last man in the world she'd ever want as a husband. She'd never be able to trust him!

And she'd be the last woman *he'd* ever want, if his gibes in the past were anything to go by...

Elizabeth Duke was born in Adelaide, South Australia, but has lived in Melbourne all her married life. She trained as a librarian and has worked in many different types of libraries, but she was always secretly writing. Her first published book was a children's novel, after which she successsfully tried her hand at romance writing. She has since given up her work as a librarian to write romance full-time. When she isn't writing or reading, she loves to travel with her husband John, either within Australia or overseas, gathering inspiration and background material for future romances. She and John have a married son and daughter, who now have children of their own.

Recent titles by the same author:

THE MARRIAGE PACT

LOOK-ALIKE FIANCÉE

BY
ELIZABETH DUKE

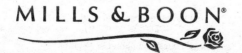

MILLS & BOON®

To Bryan
With many thanks for providing the background
for this book and for answering my endless questions,
as well as offering some brilliant suggestions of your own.

*All the characters in this book have no existence outside the imagination
of the author, and have no relation whatsoever to anyone bearing the
same name or names. They are not even distantly inspired by any
individual known or unknown to the author, and all the incidents are
pure invention.*

*First published in Great Britain 1998
Harlequin Mills & Boon Limited,
Eton House, 18-24 Paradise Road, Richmond, Surrey TW9 1SR*

© Elizabeth Duke 1998

ISBN 0 263 81149 2

*Set in Times Roman 10½ on 11¼ pt.
02-9809-55457 C1*

*Printed and bound in Norway
by AiT Trondheim AS, Trondheim*

CHAPTER ONE

IT WAS wonderfully cool and peaceful in the pine forest. The only sounds were the clear flute-like calls of the bellbirds and the swish of dry pine needles beneath Ginger's hooves. Taryn sat back in the saddle with a contented sigh, letting her fingers relax on the reins.

It was a mistake.

A kangaroo hopped out of the pines, causing Ginger to rear in fright. It happened so abruptly, so unexpectedly that it was too late for Taryn to grab hold of the reins, too late to save herself. She was already hurtling backward out of the saddle.

She landed flat on her back in a cushion of prickly pine needles.

For a second she lay with her eyes closed, trying to gather her scattered wits. She'd suffered no injury, she was sure of it. Nothing hurt. Nothing was broken. And yet...

Why did she have the feeling that she was floating...drifting away on a cloud of euphoria...dreaming a beautiful dream? Dreaming that firm, warm lips were pressing against hers...tasting...lingering...relishing...

Her eyes fluttered open.

She *was* dreaming. Or, if not dreaming, *drowning*. Drowning in a tropical blue-green sea, stabbed with pinpricks of gold.

'Well...it worked,' said a deep velvet-soft voice.

Her lips parted, her eyes slowly focusing on the deeply bronzed face above her. She *must* be dreaming. Or else she'd died and gone to heaven. Could any mortal male be this good-looking? Firm-jawed, straight-nosed,

5

suntanned...a very masculine face, full of strength and character. And breath-stopping sex appeal.

And those eyes! She felt herself drowning in them all over again, swallowed in a swirl of turquoise and jade.

'What worked?' Her lips formed the question, barely more than a husky whisper. He'd woven some kind of magic spell...was that what he meant?

'Kissing you awake. It worked for Sleeping Beauty. I thought it might work for you.' He brushed her hair away from her face, before idly winding a glossy black strand round his finger.

She blushed. Which was a first. Taryn Conway, *blushing*.

The realisation that she was passively lying on the ground *blushing*—reacting to a man she didn't even know, a man who shouldn't even be there—shattered the spell.

The dream disintegrated. She wriggled away and sat up abruptly, jerking her hair from his fingers.

'Who are *you*?' She assumed her most withering tone. Not just to cover her blushes, but to cover the stark awareness that she was alone in a shadowy, deserted forest, deep in Victoria's Strzelecki Ranges, with a complete stranger. *What was he doing, skulking around in a privately owned forest, jumping out at people?*

'I might ask you the same question.' He leaned back on his haunches, his glinting aqua eyes steady on hers. He was wearing faded jeans stretched tight over solid thighs, heavy leather boots, and a blue bush shirt with rolled-up sleeves, slashed open at the front. She averted her eyes from the skin-prickling glimpse of deeply tanned flesh and hard muscle.

'You do realise you're trespassing?' She bravely eye-balled him, hoping her crisp, quelling tone would have its usual effect. She'd used it a hundred times before to crush men who deserved to be crushed. Men who were only attracted to her, she suspected, because of her family name and her father's wealth.

He lifted a dark, taunting eyebrow. No sign of any crumbling in this man. She was the one who had to steel herself against the impact of those startling eyes. Not that she showed any reaction...not by so much as a flicker.

Now that they were at eye-level, a metre or so apart—she was still sitting, her hands curled round knees drawn up defensively in front of her—she had the chance to examine him more closely. More clinically. If it was possible to be clinical about a man with eyes that could stop a girl's heartbeat.

She noted the powerful shoulders, the strong brown arms, the way his dark hair fell in unruly waves over his brow and ears—he was in dire need of both a comb and a haircut—and the hint of raw strength in the man's well-muscled, super-fit frame.

She felt her heart give a disconcerting jump, and wasn't sure if it was a flutter of fear—or admiration. At arm's length he looked tougher, rougher, more dangerous...the blue-green eyes appearing sharper, bolder, more unnerving...nowhere near as mesmerising or as dreamlike as they'd been up close. The thick eyebrows seemed even thicker and fiercer, and there was a steely ruggedness about the stranger's strong jaw that suggested he would be a formidable foe in any fight.

What hope would *she* have against him? She might be able to handle a horse—although she had doubts about even that after her ignominious tumble a moment ago—but she had grave misgivings about her hopes of fighting off this man in a struggle.

She felt her bones dissolving at the thought of him overpowering her. But it wasn't so much fear making her weak as a devilish, heart-racing excitement...the kind of excitement she felt when she urged her mount towards a seemingly impossible jump…the thrill of facing a danger that was truly challenging, and worth facing.

It was a feeling new to her. Dangerously new.

'Trespassing?' he repeated, his tone more sardonic, she noted edgily, than defensive. 'I've been riding up in this forest for years, and this is the first time anyone's accused me of trespassing.'

'*Riding?*' she echoed, glancing round. 'I don't see your horse anywhere.' Even Ginger had deserted her, she realised in alarm. Where *was* he? Not that Fernlea was all that far away. She could always walk back if necessary. If this wild-haired stranger gave her the chance…

A shivery sensation brushed down her spine.

'I left Caesar in the orchard. You do know about the orchard?' he enquired coolly.

She lifted her chin, feeling her control slipping and this brazen *trespasser* gaining the upper hand. What did he mean, he'd been riding up here for years? Not in the past year he hadn't. Who *was* he?

'I know there's an old fruit orchard in the forest— yes.' She scrambled to her feet, deciding she was at a disadvantage sitting on the ground. 'What were you doing there? Stealing fruit?'

'*Stealing* fruit?' Scorn spiked his voice as he rose to his feet too, causing her to step back, her hand fluttering to her throat. 'I've been picking fruit up here for as long as I've been riding up here. The powers-that-be at the paper company don't mind. They're happy for the residents around here to keep an eye on the forest and help maintain the fire breaks. If they weren't, they'd have fenced it all off.'

'The *residents*?' she echoed weakly, feeling doubly weak now that he was towering over her. She took another step back, assuming her quelling tone again to bite out, 'You don't live around here!' She'd met all the locals who did. '*Do* you?' she added uncertainly, noting the mocking curve of his lips.

'I haven't lived here for a while, no, but my home's here and my father's a long-time resident. Who are *you*?' he rapped without enlightening her further. 'An over-zealous forest ranger? An employee of the paper company? If not, then *you*—if you wish to quibble about it—are trespassing yourself!'

She drew herself up to her full height of five feet six inches. Which was still several inches below the square jaw above her.

'I *own* this forest,' she said imperiously. 'At least, my family does.'

His eyes turned to glinting aqua slits. 'You're saying Gippsland Paper has *sold* this pine forest? To your family?'

'That's right. My father made them an offer and they accepted.' She felt a momentary qualm as something dark and dangerous flared in his eyes. 'They've been selling off some of their smaller plantations, and this one wasn't of much use to them anyway—it's never been thinned out. Access would have been difficult too, with all those heavily timbered hills behind and no roads. They were happy to get rid of it, I think.'

'Your *father* bought it, you said.' Now there was pure ice in his eyes. 'Your father wouldn't happen to be Hugh Conway, the city big shot who bought Fernlea a year ago, by any chance?' He waved a hand in the general direction of the hill opposite, across the sweeping green valley.

She shivered at the biting contempt in his voice. 'My father did buy Fernlea...yes.' From here, deep in the pine forest, the gabled two-storey house on the high side of the opposite hill wasn't visible, though there was a clear view of the pine forest from the house. 'You have some problem with that?'

He gave a mirthless smile. 'I knew it was too good to be true. A fairy-tale beauty with raven hair and stunning black eyes and a face and figure you only see in your dreams... There had to be a catch.'

'A catch?' She heard the huskiness in her voice, and winced. Normally comments on her looks left her unmoved. She'd been fêted and fawned over all her life—either for her looks or her father's money—and had come to mistrust extravagant compliments. She was never sure if they were genuine or merely empty flattery because of who she was.

But this man, she had a feeling, wouldn't be the type to indulge in meaningless flattery. Back-handed compliments would be more his style.

'If you're Hugh Conway's daughter, you can't be the girl of my dreams,' he said flatly, cynicism hardening his voice. 'The girl of my dreams would never be a pampered city socialite, with a doting daddy who lavishes more money and worldly possessions on his daughter than she needs or is good for her.'

She seared him with a glance, anger hiding a quick flare of hurt. A pampered *socialite*? How her mother would laugh at that! Her horse-mad, country-loving daughter preferring the high life in the city? That would be the day! As for *pampered*, she'd always been determined not to let her father's wealth or the privileges that came with it go to her head...vowing never to become the spoilt, superficial creature this man obviously thought she was. It had made her rather cool and aloof instead, except with friends she trusted.

Only now her coolness had deserted her.

'My you do have a chip on your shoulder,' she bit back. 'Do you always leap to conclusions about the people you meet?'

'Only when their name is Conway.' He tilted his head at her, his lips taking on a sardonic curl. 'I should have guessed who you were from the toffy accent. Not many people around here speak with a Toorak twang.'

She seethed inwardly, unable to refute the fact that she'd lived all her life in Melbourne's exclusive Toorak. There were, she knew, some snooty, social-climbing Toorak types who put on a studied, syrupy 'twang' purely for effect, but her own clipped, polished accent was as natural to her as breathing...she hadn't carefully cultivated it.

'What do you have against the Conways?' she hissed at him. He had a chip on his shoulder all right. A sizable one. 'Who *are* you?'

'The name's O'Malley. My father owns the dairy farm across the river from Fernlea.'

'You're Patrick O'Malley's son?' Her eyes gleamed as she saw her chance to turn the tables on him. 'You're the son who turned up his nose at dairy farming, thinking it too lowly and commonplace for him—' she felt a stab of satisfaction as she said it '—and walked out, leaving his poor widowed father in the lurch?'

The icy glitter in his own eyes showed the shaft had hit home. 'Is that what my father told you? That I walked out and left him in the lurch?'

'Your father and mine aren't exactly on speaking terms—as I'm sure you must be aware.' But she didn't want to dwell on that. 'No...it's common talk around here. How your father wanted his only son—you—to help him run the family dairy farm once you'd qualified as a vet, but you chucked your course to join a chemical company and study engineering instead.'

'Chemical engineering,' he corrected her. 'And I didn't chuck vet school...I'm a qualified vet. I just didn't practise...except as a part-time emergency vet for a while.'

'Whatever.' She shrugged, not feeling he deserved an apology. 'And since then,' she ploughed on, 'you've been roaming round Australia, making money selling some kind of parasite-killing chemical…forcing your father to hire a local to help him. You broke his heart, everyone says,' she added for good measure.

The heavy brows lowered, making her wish she hadn't repeated the gossip. But he deserved it. The way he'd reviled her and her family—so unfairly—had made her want to lash back at him.

'My father may have been disappointed,' O'Malley conceded, his deep voice roughening, 'but the only time he's been *heartbroken* was when my mother died. He's backed me all the way. You shouldn't listen to idle gossip.'

'Neither should you,' she flashed back. 'You've obviously made up your mind about me—about my family—without even bothering to get to know us.'

'From what I've heard about the Conways since I came home a couple of days ago, I'm not sure I'd *want* to be bothered.'

'Oh?' She was dismayed at the stab of hurt she felt. Not so much at what he might have heard—there was always envious gossip about the Conways—but at the derision in his voice. It was a new sensation, being scorned by a man. She tossed her head, not showing her hurt. 'And just what have you heard?'

'Let's head back to the orchard, shall we, and I'll enlighten you? Hopefully we'll find our wayward mounts there.'

She swallowed a flare of pique that he'd been the one to think of the horses first, not herself. Honestly, what was wrong with her? She was usually so cool and in command of any situation she faced. But with this man she felt as if she were floundering in an uncharted sea.

Not sure she wanted to be enlightened, she swept past him, determined not to fall casually into step beside him.

But she could hear him close behind her, his heavy boots scrunching through the pine needles.

It had become darker in the forest, she realised. Much darker. Where before there'd been fleecy white clouds above with occasional bursts of sunlight, now there was a heavy blanket of ominously dark grey above and no sign of the sun. Not that it was cold. It had been hot and humid all week, with bouts of unusually heavy early-summer rain, and it was still sultry. Not that she minded the heat. She loved everything about her rustic home-away-from-home. She had everything here…peace, spectacular beauty, fresh air…and freedom.

As she headed for the old fruit orchard around which the pine forest had been planted well over a decade ago, she heard O'Malley's voice curling around her, answering the question she wished she'd never asked. Any gossip he'd picked up about the Conways was bound to be twisted, if not totally wrong.

'The story going around,' he drawled, 'is that Hugh Conway—well-known member of the Melbourne Establishment and head of the famous Conway stock-broking firm—bought Fernlea, with its thousand-odd acres, historic Federation mansion, and old English garden, to indulge his only daughter…*you*, Miss Conway.'

She shot a virulent glance over her shoulder, but she couldn't deny it. Her father *had* bought Fernlea, basically, for her.

'You wanted more room for your horses, it seems.' The lazy voice wafted after her. 'The family's previous weekend farm closer to Melbourne didn't provide enough space for your riding and jumping pursuits. Your father's prize Angus cattle were beginning to overrun the available space, so a bigger and better property had to be found.'

When she made no comment, he added languidly, 'Not that you or your parents have been living down here permanently, I gather. You've been flitting between Fernlea and the palatial family home back in Toorak...with jaunts to the luxury beach-house at Portsea and the odd trip to Paris and London and New York in between. You've spent time at international horse shows.' He paused, then drawled silkily, 'I'm sure you sit a horse beautifully, Miss Conway.'

'I thought it was only women who lapped up gossip,' she snapped over her shoulder. 'You've been back home for barely two days and you think you know all there is to know about us! Well, you've told me more than I'll ever want to know about *you*, Mr O'Malley. You should do something about that chip on your shoulder. It's most unattractive!'

'If I have one, it's with good reason.'

Her step faltered. 'Meaning?'

'Forget it. Are Mummy and Daddy down here with you?' he asked blandly.

She gritted her teeth and answered levelly, 'My parents had to go back to town this morning, but they'll be down again on Friday for a few days.'

'Well...so for now you're lady of the manor? Literally.'

Her eyes wavered. 'What do you mean—literally?'

'Fernlea—as I'm sure you already know—was once one of the grand old homes of Gippsland. Some of the old English oaks and elms in the garden are over a hundred years old. You must have great fun swanning around your grand estate, throwing house parties for your socialite pals!'

'It might have been a grand old home once,' she flashed back, 'but it was badly in need of repair when we bought it.' A fractious frown creased her brow. He made it sound as if her father had bought Fernlea simply to indulge a spoilt daughter's whim...as if it were no more to her than a diverting hobby farm or weekend retreat. How wrong he was! 'We've been gradually repairing and renovating the place over time...'

'Sparing no expense, I'm sure.'

'Meanwhile,' she said, ignoring his comment, 'it's quite livable. Peeling paint and frayed curtains and a sagging, rusty roof are not things that greatly bother me,' she assured him tartly. 'There were lots of other more urgent things that needed doing first. Like mending fences and clearing away the choking blackberries and fixing up the run-down stables and levelling off an area for a jumping course and—'

'And buying up old Henderson's property, Plane Tree Flats, to add to your domain...even though it's on *our* side of the river and of more use to us.' The contempt was back in his voice.

Her head jerked round. 'You're saying that *you*—the O'Malleys—wanted to buy that piece of land?'

'That's right. It used to belong to my family—until a bushfire and drought nearly wiped us out when I was a boy, forcing my father to sell off that chunk of land. Dad's been wanting to buy it back for years. When the chance came,' he ground out, 'Hugh Conway swanned in with a higher offer and we lost out.'

'So that's why you hate us,' Taryn breathed. She stopped and swung round, planting her hands on her hips. As she raised her eyes to his face, she swallowed. Hard. It was so dark in the forest by now that the granite-hard face under the mass of dark hair looked positively frightening, causing her heart to skip in sudden panic. If he hated her so much...

'We were trying to *help* Charley Henderson,' she offered in her father's defence, aware that her voice sounded annoyingly husky. 'The old man was badly in debt and in very poor health. He needed to be closer to town and hospital care. Now he'll be able to live comfortably for the rest of his life, with the best of medical care at his fingertips.'

'Oh, I'm sure your father was acting out of the goodness of his heart when he bought that prime piece of land over our heads,' O'Malley bit back with scorn. 'What good is it to you? It's on the other side of the river, with no access from your property!'

'There will be. We're building a bridge across the river.'

'Of course. Naturally. And I'm sure it will be a state-of-the-art concrete bridge too, not a rickety old thing like the one between your property and ours. Which is likely to wash away, incidentally, if we get any more heavy rain. The river normally fades to a trickle once the hot weather starts, but this year it's flowing like crazy.'

She jerked a careless shoulder. She knew about the old timber bridge over the river, where it ran between the O'Malleys' property and theirs, but with the ill feeling between the two families it would hardly matter if it did wash away. It was unlikely that either family would want to use it anyway.

'Talking of heavy rain… ' O'Malley glanced up at the sky '…I'd say that's just what we're about to get.'

She glanced up too, and stifled a groan. The sky looked even more threatening now, and she could hear thunder rumbling in the distance. She quickened her steps.

'You didn't answer my question,' O'Malley growled from behind. 'What do *you* want with Charley Henderson's land? Do you intend to run cattle there? Horses? Will you be pulling down Henderson's old house?'

'My father will be running cattle there. It's extremely fertile land on Plane Tree Flats, as you must know…in that wide loop of the river. And no, we won't be pulling down the old house—if it's any of your business. The young couple we hired to help us run Fernlea will be living there. They've been coming from Leongatha every day, but we want them to live here on the property so they can keep a closer eye on the place when we're not here. Like Smudge does…your father's right-hand man, who lives on *your* property.'

She flicked a glance round to add sweetly, 'I heard about Smudge from the young couple who work for us, not from your father. Your father hasn't been particularly neighbourly.' She paused, then asked idly, 'Does he dislike us because we made a higher offer for Charley Henderson's old farm? Or does he have a chip on his shoulder about the Conways too…no matter what we do?'

'Put it this way,' O'Malley said, his tone curt. 'Neither of us cares overmuch for weekend *hobby* farmers. And now you tell me that the Conways, not content with owning Fernlea and Plane Tree Flats, have bought this pine forest as well!'

'You're saying that you O'Malleys wanted the pine forest as well as Plane Tree Flats?'

'If we'd known the Conways were after it,' came the grating response, 'we might have tried to prevent the sale. You're aware, I hope, that it's an environmental gem in these parts? The residents around here have enjoyed the use of this forest and the old fruit orchard for years. What do *you* intend to do with it? Raze it to the ground?'

'Of course not! We want to keep it just the way it is…that's precisely why we bought it. Our property *overlooks* the forest. We had no wish to see it logged one day.'

'Ah! So you bought it so that your pleasant *view* wouldn't be spoiled. Of course…why didn't I guess? Next you'll be fencing it all off, with padlocked gates, so that nobody else can get near the forest *or* the orchard. Right?'

'Wrong!' She could feel her cheeks burning. Her father *had* suggested fencing the forest. To *protect* it, not to keep the neighbours out. 'The farmers who live around here will be welcome to keep coming up here,' she spelt out, 'so long as they're careful and don't light fires or drop cigarettes around.'

'The farmers around here don't light fires. They *protect* against fires. They help to maintain the fire breaks around the forest and they watch out for lightning strikes that might *start* a fire...or for people who shouldn't be here. That's why I left my horse in the orchard and followed you. To see what you were up to. Only to find that you Conways have *bought* the forest and want to keep it to yourselves!'

'You can still ride up here,' she protested in a muffled voice. Each word he uttered flayed a sensitive part of her that she'd never realised existed. It had never particularly bothered her before what people thought of her. But for some odd reason—some *stupid* reason, in light of his attitude—she cared what *this* man thought.

Because he was a close neighbour? Was that the only reason she cared? All she knew was that, despite his abrasive manner and the giant chip on his shoulder and his obvious loathing of people with money, she didn't want him to loathe *her*.

'You told me I was trespassing,' he reminded her.

She swallowed. 'I didn't know who you were then. You—you could have been a firebug, for all I knew.'

They were in the overgrown orchard by now, weaving their way through the old fruit trees...apples, pears, apricots, quinces...even a giant mulberry tree. She glimpsed Ginger ahead, nose to the ground, munching fallen apples. A whinnying sound snapped her head round. Standing nearby, pawing at the ground, was another horse. A magnificent creature with a shiny black coat and a flowing black mane. He seemed high-strung and nervous…spooked, perhaps, by the thunder.

'No sudden movements,' O'Malley hissed at her ear. 'Caesar's easily startled. He hates storms. Let's approach nice and easy… You grab your horse first.'

As she approached Ginger, a flash of lightning lit up the pines. Just as she caught the gelding's reins in her fingers, an explosive bang shook the earth, causing Ginger to jerk back in fright. But this time she had a tight grip on the reins and was able to control him within seconds, patting him and murmuring soothing words.

'Hey! Come back here!'

Her head whipped round as O'Malley roared at Caesar and lunged forward. But he was too late. Caesar was bolting off down the hill, black mane flying, deaf to O'Malley's shouts.

She bit her lip, repressing a giggle. She couldn't help it. Served him right! Now he'd have to walk back…and to reach his father's dairy farm from here would be a hike-and-a-half on foot!

A moment later her grin was wiped from her lips as the heavens opened and the rain came bucketing down, soaking her to the skin in seconds. Her hair, streaming with water, clung to her shoulders. Watery drops trickled down her neck and inside the collar of her shirt.

O'Malley, looking just as bedraggled, his wild hair now flattened to his head, hiding his heavy eyebrows, cursed audibly. 'My father should have got rid of that damned horse years ago. Caesar never listens, never does what you want.'

'You should be soulmates, then,' she tossed back, unable to resist having another shot at him for ignoring his father's wishes. 'I'm sure your father would agree.'

He glowered at her. 'My father and I—' he began, and stopped abruptly. She saw an amazing change come over his face. The irate frown dissolved. The chilly eyes took on a soulfully pleading expression, the gruffness in his voice giving way to a playfully wheedling note.

'You're not going to make me walk all the way home in this filthy rain, are you?'

CHAPTER TWO

SHE blinked at him. 'You can't mean—' She glanced from O'Malley to the saddle on Ginger's back. He had to be joking!

'After all your talk about being neighbourly,' he cajoled, as another blinding flash lit the sky, 'I thought you might offer me a ride back to the old timber bridge… through Fernlea. It would take me hours to walk back the long way…the way I came up.'

Thunder rocketed across the valley. Ginger threw up his head, nearly dragging the reins from Taryn's clutching fingers. She felt O'Malley's hand on hers as he snatched the reins from her, steadying the horse with an iron grip.

'We'd better get out of this forest…fast,' he gritted, 'before we're struck by lightning.' Water was pouring down his face, beading his eyelashes. 'Are you going to give me a ride or not?' He appealed to her with the full force of his glittering gaze. 'Or do you want me to end up with pneumonia…or drowned?'

His shirt was almost transparent, clinging to his tightly muscled chest and powerful arms like a second skin. She tried not to think about what her own sodden shirt might be revealing.

She really had no choice. How could she leave him stranded up here in a thunderstorm, in pouring rain, a long, muddy walk from his home?

'Let's go, then,' she mumbled, blinking away the drops of water gathering on her own lashes.

'You mount first,' he said without ado. Not even a 'thank you', she noticed. 'I'll climb up behind.'

21

Behind? She could feel her wet cheeks sizzling as he gave her a hand up, then hauled himself up behind her. Far too close behind...his powerful arms curving around her, cocooning her in the relative shelter of his all-too-male, strongly muscled frame.

She swallowed hard, chewing on her lip, fighting down an almost uncontrollable trembling. *What was wrong with her?* There was nothing personal about this...he was just using her...saving himself a long tramp home in the rain.

'You hold the reins...I'll hold onto you,' O'Malley shouted over the rain, and she nodded, heat still firing her cheeks.

Neither spoke—other than to shout a command or a soothing word at Ginger—as they steered the big gelding out of the orchard, through the dripping pines to the ploughed fire break skirting the forest. Luckily, the carpet of fallen pine needles had prevented the track turning completely to mud, and before long they were heading downhill, following the steep track they would both have taken coming up. It was very slippery and dangerous now, needing all their concentration.

Several times, as Ginger missed his footing and almost fell, she felt O'Malley's grip tighten round her waist, his strong hands clamping round her like a vice. She wasn't sure if it was to save her...or himself. She only knew that her breath quickened each time it happened.

Further down the hill the track branched into two...one following the heavily timbered slopes round—way round—to the O'Malleys' sprawling dairy farm, the other passing through the Conways' extensive property, which lay spread out over the hills ahead.

'There's no sign of your horse,' Taryn shouted as they crossed a narrow creek—which, she knew, ran into the river further round. The upper part of an old railway carriage had been dumped in the creekbed to form a bridge.

'Don't worry about Caesar.' O'Malley's deep voice rolled through her. 'He's like a homing pigeon. He'll be back home by now, under shelter. Lucky devil.'

They were climbing again now, water spraying from Ginger's hooves as the rain continued to tumble down, though at least it was no longer bucketing down in a solid, deafening sheet. The sky remained low and black, with bright flashes from time to time, and rolling thunder in the distance.

Eventually they reached a gate and came to a halt.

'I'll open it,' O'Malley offered, sliding from Ginger's rump, taking the warmth and comfort of his arms and solid frame with him. Taryn was aware of a slight chill without his sheltering presence close behind her.

As she guided Ginger through the open gate, O'Malley squinted up at her, as if he half expected her to keep on riding, leaving him to shut the gate after her and tramp the long way back to his home on foot. She muffled a sigh as she pulled up and waited for him. How little he thought of her!

She didn't glance round at him as he mounted behind her after closing the gate. 'Go, Ginger!' she urged, almost before O'Malley was settled on the gelding's back. Her face was taut. He was never going to think well of her—of a Conway—whatever she did. The sooner she was rid of him the better!

Narrowing her eyes against the rain, she saw the house and outbuildings ahead, partially masked by a row of huge cypresses. She was longing to get out of the soaking rain into clean dry clothes...longing to get back to the privacy and tranquillity of her comfortable country home. But she knew she'd have to take O'Malley to *his* home first, taking the short cut to his property across the old timber bridge over the river, down the hill below Fernlea.

She needn't, she decided, take him all the way to his house, which she knew was way up on the crest of the hill. As soon as she was reasonably close, she would drop him off, turn tail, and go. They'd both be glad to see the back of each other!

But would she really be glad, deep down? She chewed on her lip. If only he weren't so…so infuriatingly, heart-tuggingly attractive. If only her mind wasn't seething with questions about him. Why had he come back? How long did he intend to stay? Had he changed his mind about dairy farming and decided to come home for good?

If he had, he would be her neighbour. A *close* neighbour.

Once he came to know her better, would he bury his prejudices and grievances against the Conways? Would his *father*? Or would they both remain antagonistic…persisting with this pernicious, rather puerile O'Malley-Conway feud?

Neither attempted to make conversation as Ginger ploughed on in the rain, heading towards the old timber bridge over the river now, rather than the sheltering haven of Fernlea. They needed to concentrate on where they were treading, and besides, the rain running into their eyes and mouths made normal conversation difficult.

When they finally came in sight of the oak-lined river, Taryn let out an audible groan.

'The bridge! What's happened to it?'

Stupid question. It was obvious that the rain—or rather, the gushing torrent—had swept away the rotting timber supports that had once spanned the river, leaving only a few straggly pieces of wood behind. If the river hadn't been running so high, or so fiercely, it might have been possible for an athletic man to cross it by leaping from log to log, but at the moment it was impassable!

'What are you going to do?' she croaked, deliberately not saying 'we'. This was O'Malley's problem, not hers. It would take him hours to tramp back the way he'd come, along the track below the forest...and even longer by road, without a car.

'If you'll take me back to your house, Miss Conway,' O'Malley suggested coolly, 'I'll call my father—if you'll permit me—and ask him to come and pick me up in the ute.'

Her head snapped round. 'You can't expect your father to drive all the way here in this weather! It'll be too hard to see. Too dangerous. He might run off the road.'

For a brief second their eyes met. She caught a faint gleam in the sharp blue. 'Well...when the rain eases off a bit,' he compromised. 'If you won't mind giving me shelter in the meantime.'

She turned away sharply so that he couldn't see how appalled she was at the idea of sheltering O'Malley in her home until the rain stopped. That might be hours! It was late afternoon already.

'I'll run you home myself,' she rapped out, 'in the four-wheel drive. It's in the garage...this way.' Jerking at the reins, she prodded Ginger with her knees.

'No, you won't.' O'Malley's voice rumbled at her ear. 'The roads will be awash right now...especially the unsealed sections. If it's too dangerous for my father, it will be too dangerous for you.'

'I'm much younger than your—'

'Forget it. Look, let's just get out of this rain. We'll fight it out later.'

For the second time that afternoon, she had no choice. He was right. The sooner they were out of this lousy rain the better. She wasn't even warm any more, despite the humidity in the air. She could feel the dampness chilling her to the bone.

With a shrug, she pointed Ginger in the direction of the stables...an old two-storey barn which had been there, she'd learned from old photographs they'd found in a cupboard, for as long as the house. The building was in need of repair, like everything else, but provided adequate shelter meantime, and the roomy loft above, when done up, would make ideal accommodation for guests or future stable hands.

Once there, she was tempted to stay put. The stables seemed safer, somehow, than the house, and at least they were under cover, out of the rain. She looked hopefully up at the sky, but there was no sign as yet of any lightening in the cloud cover, or any real slackening in the rain.

'Are we going to make a dash for the house?' O'Malley said finally. 'You should get out of those wet clothes. I'll stay out on the verandah if you don't want to invite me in.'

You should get out of those wet clothes...

Her eyes leapt to his. What did she expect to see? A leer? Carnal intent? A lecherous glint as his imagination went haywire, evoking images of her removing her sodden shirt and jeans?

All she saw was cool, dispassionate reason. He was right. Again. As usual.

'Right,' she mumbled. 'P-perhaps you'd like some coffee while we're waiting for the rain to—' she nearly said 'stop', but that might take hours '—to ease off,' she said instead.

'Thanks. Let's make a dash, then,' he rapped, and they both sprinted towards the house, not pausing until they reached the vine-covered verandah.

She hesitated as she thrust her key in the kitchen door. 'Do you want me to bring your coffee out to you?' she

asked in a stilted voice. How could she invite him inside? Not only was he dripping wet, but her parents
would have a fit if they found out she'd invited a virtual
stranger into the house while she was down here alone.
He might be the son of a neighbour, but he was still a
stranger. And being an O'Malley, a *hostile* stranger.

'I don't suppose you'd have a clothes dryer?'
O'Malley enquired hopefully.

Her throat went dry. 'Why?' she asked warily, hoping
he didn't mean what she thought he meant. But what
else *could* he mean?

'*Have* you? I can't imagine the Conways not having
all mod cons.'

She sucked in a deep, quivering breath. Another sly
dig at the Conways! He just couldn't resist. She glowered up at him. 'We have...as a matter of fact. But if
you think—'

'What I'd really like,' O'Malley cut in, spreading his
hands as if to say, Look at me...look at the state I'm in,
'is a shower...if you have a spare one in a back room
or outhouse somewhere. These wet clothes feel damned
uncomfortable. You could throw my clothes in the dryer
and they'd be dry by the time we'd finished our coffee.'

A suffocating sensation threatened to crush her, to
squeeze all the air from her lungs. 'You—you intend to
get *undressed*?' She stared at him. Trying not to imagine
how he'd look if he did. A sight to behold, she traitor-
ously thought, heat flaming through her.

He's an O'Malley, she thought wildly. *He despises
you and everything you stand for. He won't try anything.*

Or maybe that was the very reason he would!

'It would be difficult to dry my wet clothes without
undressing first,' he pointed out reasonably. 'Naturally,
I'd disrobe in private.' His eyes glinted wickedly, as if
he'd read her mind a second ago.

'I should hope so!' she hissed, thinning her lips and

glaring at him to hide the burning mortification she felt inside. 'Th-there's a shower in the washroom...just along the verandah, second door along. You can use that. Wait here and I'll unlock the door from inside.'

As she kicked off her muddy boots and let herself into the kitchen, he called after her. 'I'd be grateful if you'd lend me a towel. An old one will do. And maybe...' amused irony licked through his voice '...one of your father's monogrammed smoking jackets, if that would be less likely to offend your sensibilities.'

She paused, gritting her teeth. She didn't trust herself to turn round. She knew his eyes would be mocking her, if not openly laughing at her.

'The chip on your shoulder's showing again,' she snapped. 'Or is it *envy*? You have a secret longing for a monogrammed smoking jacket? I'll see what I can find!' She let the door slam behind her.

A few minutes later she jerked open the outer wash-room door. Peeking out, she saw O'Malley patiently waiting on the verandah, lolling against one of the vine-clad timber posts.

'You can come in now.' Avoiding his eye as he strode towards her, she thrust a bulging sports bag at him. 'You'll find a towel and something to wear in here.' She kept her head down to hide the mischievous glint in her eye.

'Thanks, ma'am. This is real neighbourly of you.'

Was that another dig? Or an apology of sorts...know-ing that his father was less than neighbourly and wouldn't even speak to them?

'Throw your things into the dryer,' she said briskly, 'and when you're ready come to the kitchen.' She would put her own wet clothes into the washing machine later. 'You know where the kitchen door is.' Let him come in from the verandah, not through the house. 'Enjoy your shower!' She swung away before he could catch the impish smile on her lips.

She raced upstairs to the main bathroom next to her big double bedroom overlooking the vast tree-lined lawn.

Being such an old house, it had no *en suites* off the bedrooms, though the rooms were large enough to put them in at a later stage. Her father had wanted to modernise the bedrooms and put spa baths in the planned *en suites*, but she'd insisted the rooms must be renovated in the authentic old Federation style, with old-style *en suites* to match, and no modern spas. And, since she would be spending the most time here at Fernlea, her father had bowed to her wishes.

O'Malley, no doubt, would see it differently. He'd see it as the pampered daughter getting her own way again. Getting whatever she wanted.

She caught a glimpse of herself in the mirror. What a sight! She looked like a drowned bush rat! Where was the pampered socialite now? *Socialite!* She snorted, her lip curling. O'Malley had a lot to learn!

She showered and dressed in double-quick time, throwing on a clean white T-shirt and her oldest, most faded pair of jeans. She wanted to avoid giving O'Malley a chance to taunt her for wearing expensive designer jeans or a famous-label shirt. Not that she didn't possess such items…she did…mostly picked up at sales, and only well-cut, top-quality gear that she knew would last better than the cheaper variety.

She pulled back her still damp, shoulder-length hair into a ponytail, securing it with a black scrunchie. She left her face bare of make-up, not even bothering with lipstick. Her lips were full enough and pink enough to get away without lipstick, and her lashes, being as thick and black as her hair, needed no enhancing.

It was just as well she hadn't been wearing make-up

earlier, she mused, or her mascara would have run down her cheeks and her lipstick would have been smeared across her chin! She could just imagine how O'Malley would have teased her about *that*!

She suppressed a giggle as she ran down the stairs to the kitchen. Now she was going to get her chance to laugh at *him*!

There was no sign of him as yet. She set about preparing the coffee, filling the pot and taking two mugs from hooks on the wall. It was a big old country-style kitchen with cupboards and benches lining the walls and a long table in the middle, with several chairs. She'd recently made new curtains and given the walls a new coat of paint.

She heard O'Malley's voice at the door. 'Hullo there.'

'Come in,' she called, glancing round, biting her lip in wicked expectation.

Her eyes bulged as O'Malley stepped into the kitchen, her face flaming as she saw that he'd outsmarted her. All he was wearing was a skimpy white towel, wrapped round his waist!

'Wh-what happened to the dressing-gown I gave you?' she squeaked, her eyes riveted for a stunned second to his bare, bronzed chest and powerful tanned legs. 'I... It was the nearest thing I had to a—a smoking jacket.'

'Pink's not my colour.' He shrugged, and spread his hands—both of them, causing her to bite back a gasp and jerk her head away, expecting the towel to unravel. 'And it was a bit tight and flimsy across the shoulders. I didn't want to rip it and incur your wrath. It's obviously your very best negligée.'

She hissed in her breath. 'I've never worn it,' she growled, attending to the coffee as if her life depended on it. 'My mother gave it to me. She likes frilly, frivolous things. I don't.'

'I'm sure it would look charming on *you*,' he demurred, and she could almost feel his eyes undressing her.

'I just keep it for guests,' she muttered, her hand unsteady as she poured the coffee. *Female* guests—though she would have given anything to have seen O'Malley prancing around in it, frills and all. She felt a giggle bubbling to her lips.

'You must have some very odd male guests,' he commented gravely. 'I've often wondered how you social set get your kicks.'

She flounced round, thrusting his mug of coffee at him. 'OK, so you called my bluff,' she scratched out. 'Let's drop it, shall we?' She snatched in a horrified breath as his hand moved to the towel. *'No! Not the towel!'* She shut her eyes. 'Look, I'll go and find you something else to wear…'

He caught her arm as she tried to dash past him. 'No need. I'm not cold. Sit down and have your coffee. Haven't you ever seen a naked male chest before?'

'It—it's not that—' She snapped her mouth shut, horrified at the way she was stammering. It was so unlike her. Normally nothing fazed her.

'It's not my chest?' he enquired blandly, pulling out a chair.

She held her breath and averted her gaze as he lowered himself down.

'Look, if it's any help,' he drawled, sounding amused, 'I've a pair of boxer shorts under the towel. The ones you threw in with the negligée.' He paused. 'One of your male guests must have left them behind.'

She sank into the chair opposite, relief trickling through her. She'd forgotten about the boxer shorts. 'They—they're my father's…and they're new. They were still in their original pack. I—I didn't think he'd mind.'

'I trust not. I felt I should avail myself of them…if only to save your blushes.' Tilting his head at her, he added musingly, 'You know, I expected Hugh Conway's daughter to be older and more—' he pursed his lips '—more hard-boiled. More the jaded, seen-it-all-done-it-all sophisticate. Are you really as young and ingenuous as you seem? You look about sixteen.'

Sixteen! Sparks lit her eyes. This was *too* much!

'I'm twenty-three years old,' she snapped, 'and I've just finished an arts degree at university.'

'Goodness…twenty-three!' Mock wonder danced in his eyes. She clenched her hands into fists, realising he'd teased her into blurting out the truth. 'And an arts degree, eh? Well done. Not just a pretty face, then.' The edges of his mouth twitched. 'Perhaps not the idle, empty-headed socialite I imagined.'

Her fingernails dug into her flesh. He didn't have to sound so surprised! 'Are you being condescending because I'm the pampered Conway girl,' she grated, 'or are you always this patronising with women?'

'I was *congratulating* you.' He defended himself with an injured expression. 'Do you intend to go on with your studies?' he asked pleasantly. 'There's not much one can do these days with an arts degree on its own…'

'I realise that, but no, I won't be doing any more study for now. I'll be too busy. It was just an interest, to keep my mind active.' *Damn,* she thought. *That sounds so smug and self-indulgent! No wonder he thinks I'm a bored, pampered socialite with nothing better to do!*

She lifted her coffee mug and drained the contents, avoiding his eye. 'I compete in horse shows, which means lots of training and travelling around,' she told him, keeping her voice steady with an effort. She shouldn't care what this insufferable man thought of her, but for some reason she did! 'It meant I could only go to uni part-time, so I took longer to get my degree.'

'So it was more of a part-time *hobby*...between horse shows,' he murmured, 'than a serious, full-time commitment with a professional career in mind?' He nodded, as if it was no more than he expected. 'You're more interested in parading around the arena with your peers. Gathering ribbons. Gathering applause. That's where your ambition lies.'

There was a new note in his voice, a coldly cynical note that raised her hackles.

She scraped back her chair. 'My *ambition*,' she said through gritted teeth, 'is to compete in the Sydney Olympic Games. Not just compete, but hopefully to win a gold medal for Australia!' She jerked to her feet and stepped over to the bench. 'More coffee?' Rain was still drumming on the roof. She had an unhappy feeling that she was stuck with him for some time yet.

'Thanks, I will.'

As she reached for the coffee pot, he added smoothly, 'Well...the Olympics, eh? That's some ambition. And aiming for gold...for the top...I'm impressed.' If he'd only stopped there she might have believed him. But of course he didn't. Not O'Malley.

'Is it likely to happen?' he asked, a bantering note in his voice now. 'Or just wishful thinking?'

He didn't think she was serious about her lofty ambition...let alone believe for one second that she would ever *reach* such an exalted standard. To him, she was the pampered socialite to whom everything came easily. The spoilt rich girl who'd had everything handed to her on a silver platter. To reach Olympic standard would mean hard work...sacrifice...a long, tough, arduous grind. Words the cosseted Conway girl wouldn't know!

Well, I'll show you, O'Malley, she vowed under her breath. *One of these days you'll come grovelling...begging my forgiveness for having doubted me.*

The thought of O'Malley grovelling to anyone was a

diverting thought. Not that she could imagine it happening in the next million years!

'You'd cut quite a dash, I'd imagine,' O'Malley drawled, his tone pure velvet now, 'in tight-fitting jodhpurs and a smart nipped-in jacket, with a neat little helmet perched on your head.'

She could feel his gaze burning over her from behind, bringing a tingling warmth to her skin. And a spark of battle to her eyes. Swinging round, she stomped back to the table and poured coffee into his mug. Tempted to pour it over him. The condescending, patronising, insufferable... Words weren't strong enough to describe him!

'Thank you, Miss Conway.' He glanced up at her. 'Much obliged.'

'Taryn,' she ground out, hating that patronising 'Miss Conway'.

'Sorry?'

'Taryn. That's my name.' She poured some coffee into her own mug, annoyed at the way her hand was shaking, then turned away to replace the coffee pot on the bench, taking her mug with her. Instead of sitting down again, she strolled over to the window, staring dismally across the rain-soaked yard to the misty hills beyond. Would this wretched rain never stop? *What if it kept on until nightfall?*

She muffled a groan, trembling at the dire—very real—possibility.

'Taryn.' He repeated the name. 'Taryn Conway.' The bantering note was back in his voice. 'I might have known it wouldn't be Jane or Mary. Nothing plain or ordinary for the Conway girl. That wouldn't do, would it?'

She drew in her lips. Usually people reacted to her name with remarks like, 'What a pretty name' or 'How unusual', but O'Malley, of course, had to be different and make it into a personal attack. Not that he'd actually said he *disliked* the name. But it was obvious he thought it too elaborate, chosen purely for effect. As far as she knew, her mother had simply plucked it from a book of names because she'd liked it.

'And *your* name is…?' She cast him a withering look. Heaven help him if it was anything more unusual than Tom, Charlie, or Jack!

'Mine? Oh, you can call me Mike.'

Mike… She pursed her lips. Well, she could hardly call that elaborate or unusual. *Mike*… Michael O'Malley. It suited him, she decided, distracted for a second. Sort of tough, masculine, no frills. And very Irish. Not that he sounded the least bit Irish. But then he wouldn't. The O'Malleys, from the snippets she'd heard about them, had lived in Australia for generations.

'Won't your father be getting worried about you?' she asked tetchily. 'Especially if he happens to see your horse come back without you.'

'If my father has any sense he'll be sheltering inside out of the rain, and won't even notice if Caesar's there or not. As for Caesar, he'll head straight for his food bin and a roof over his head.'

'But he *might* be worried,' she persisted. 'You should give him a call and—and let him know you're safe.'

She felt his eyes on her. 'Your concern for my father does you credit, Miss Conway…sorry, Taryn.' He paused, slanting his head. 'Yes…the name does suit you,' he decided, but he didn't spell out why. 'All right…I'll let him know I'm here. I'll get him to send his young farmhand to pick me up in the ute. Smudge is much younger and fitter than Dad, so you won't need to be concerned about *him*.'

Something shimmered in his eyes as he said it, causing her own eyes to waver. Was he wondering if her concern for his father was genuine?

'I'd better check on my clothes,' he said, 'and see if

they're dry enough to put back on.' He rose slowly, with a sigh, as if reluctant to leave the table.

Or reluctant to let his father know he was at the Conways?

That was more like it. Patrick O'Malley had made it plain he wanted nothing to do with his new neighbours. Not simply because they were the rich, high-flying Conways—mere hobby-farmers or 'townies', as he apparently saw them—but for what he perceived they'd done to him. Buying the rich slice of land *he'd* wanted to buy. Or rather had wanted to buy *back*.

Within minutes Mike was back, fully dressed in the jeans and bush shirt he'd taken from the dryer—looking a bit crumpled, but dry. She breathed a sigh of relief. It had been getting harder and harder to avoid looking at that expanse of deeply tanned chest...the taut golden muscles...the trail of dark hair that ran—

She snapped off her thoughts.

'The phone's over there...on the wall.' She waved a hand, her heart picking up a beat as he reached for it and stabbed it several times with his finger. How would his father take it when he heard his son was here at Fernlea? At the Conway house?

'Damn.' Mike lowered the phone with a frown. 'Your phone's dead. The rain must have soaked into one of the junction boxes. Or a tree's come down somewhere.'

'Are you sure?' She grabbed it from him in disbelief. He had to be making it up! He didn't want his father knowing he was here. Or he was using it as an excuse to stay here a bit longer. *All night, perhaps?*

Over my dead body, she thought, a prickling sensation crawling along her skin.

She clamped the phone to her ear. And had to gulp in suddenly needed air. There was silence at the other end. Dead silence. She banged it with her open palm. She frantically pressed some buttons. She shook it.

'I don't think that's going to do much good,' Mike said calmly.

'We're completely cut off,' she moaned. And touched her throat with unsteady fingers, realising what it meant. Now there was no way he could let his father know he was safe. No way he could let his father know he was sheltering here at Fernlea. No way he could get his father's hired hand to come and fetch him.

Well, you're not staying here, Michael O'Malley, her eyes told him. *No way.*

CHAPTER THREE

HER gaze swivelled to the window. 'I think it's easing off,' she blurted. 'I'll take you home myself. We'll have to leave now, so I can be back before dark.' She knew she was gabbling, but she couldn't help it. 'Shall we go? I'll just grab my purse and keys.' She whirled out into the hall where she'd left them.

She expected him to argue, but he didn't. Maybe he could sense that she was in deadly earnest this time. 'Much obliged,' was all he said as she came flouncing back into the kitchen, keys and purse in hand.

She snapped on lights as she dashed out of the door, not wanting to come back to a darkened house. Dusk would be falling shortly. Even nightfall, if they didn't get a move on. Mike was right behind her, pulling the kitchen door shut after him.

'You want to lock it?' he asked, but she shook her head and plunged on. She could hear him behind her, taking long, swift strides to keep up.

She didn't pause until she reached the double garage. There were two vehicles inside, the sturdy Toyota Land Cruiser they kept down here at Fernlea for use around the property and for pulling the horse-float, and her small, zippy Ford Laser, which she used between here and the city, and for running around back in Melbourne.

'Like me to drive?' Mike offered, hovering at her shoulder as she unlocked the big four-wheel drive.

'You don't trust me to drive you?' she asked, her eyes coolly taunting him, even as her heart jumped at his closeness, her senses jangling at the faint scent of soap and freshly dried clothes.

38

'Well, I hope you don't drive as wildly as you rush around your yard,' Mike remarked dryly.

Her dark eyes took on a knife-sharp glitter. So it wasn't just a courtesy offer...or a male disliking being driven by a female. He was scared that she might land them in a ditch!

'I guess you'll just have to take the risk,' she flung back, hauling herself up into the driver's seat. He didn't lend a hand, perhaps sensing that she'd snap his head off if he tried. He stepped round to the passenger's side without further comment.

She backed out rather more quickly than she normally would, just to keep him on his toes. But once out of the yard and on the road—more a sealed lane than a road, though it would change to bitumen and widen at the old concrete bridge where the lane joined the main road—she slackened her speed and concentrated on where she was going. She had to. It was still raining, though thankfully not so heavily now, and the edges of the road were soft and slushy—to be carefully avoided if she didn't want to risk sliding off or getting bogged.

Mike didn't attempt to make conversation, obviously not wanting to spoil her concentration. Even without glancing round, she could feel the hawk-eyed tension in him, and knew that he was watching the road as attentively as she. There could be other dangers besides mud and slush. A wombat or kangaroo could emerge from the bush and cross their path. There were plenty around.

The last thing she expected to see was another car coming towards them. The road they were on led only to Fernlea. Who could be coming to visit her in this weather, she wondered, at this late hour in the day? It couldn't be her parents. They'd gone back to town only this morning to attend a special dinner tonight.

'Watch out!' rasped Mike. 'There's a car coming.'

'I can see it!' she hissed, slowing down as the two

cars drew closer. She reached down to switch her head-lights on, just in case the oncoming driver hadn't seen *her*. At once the other car's lights sprang on too, as if the driver had had the same thought.

'Who is it? Your father? It's obviously someone who knows you, since he's heading for Fernlea. Unless it's someone who's lost his way. It does happen around these parts.'

'We'll soon find out.' She brought the Land Cruiser to a halt as far to one side of the road as she could—making sure the wheels were still on the solid ground—and opened her window to signal to the other driver to pull up too.

Mike gave a soft whistle as the other car, a sleek red sports car, pulled up a few metres away—not too close, as if the driver was wary of strange four-wheel-drive vehicles that might scratch or muddy his beautiful car.

'Well...it's obviously a friend of yours,' Mike mur-mured. 'Porsches don't often appear in these parts. Or didn't until the Conways moved in down here.'

A Porsche! Taryn's stomach lurched. She only knew one person who drove a red Porsche. Rory Silverman... polo-playing playboy son of Rex Silverman, the mining tycoon. The Silvermans owned a huge property the other side of Warragul, less than ten kilometres from here. She'd met Rory at an equestrian function, and he'd rung her a few times since to ask her out. So far she'd had a ready excuse each time—he was far too smooth and full of himself for her liking—but he hadn't taken the hint.

The last time he'd called her he'd told her that he might pop over to Fernlea one day to see her. 'We must catch up with each other, Taryn,' he'd purred, 'before I go off overseas again.'

She'd hoped he'd forgotten. Or had been too busy. Or had already gone overseas.

Obviously not. No such luck.

'You stay here,' she rapped at Mike. 'I'll go and speak to him. I know who it is.'

She grabbed an umbrella from the back seat where she always kept one, and clambered out, snapping it open as she strode over to the Porsche.

The driver wound down his window. 'Taryn…it's you!'

Good-looking, tawny-haired, suave… Yes, it was Rory Silverman all right.

'Rory! I…I hope you weren't coming to visit *me*?'

What she really wanted to know was what, precisely, he'd had in mind. She compressed her lips. Why would he call on her at this late hour of the day, in this appalling weather…unless he was hoping to *stay the night*?

His long-lashed grey eyes peered up at her. 'I called you before I came,' he told her in his well-cultivated, smooth-as-silk voice, 'but there seems to be something wrong with your phone. I knew your parents would be back in town—they're going to the same dinner as mine—so I thought I'd better rush over and make sure you were all right.'

I'll bet, she thought, unconvinced at his display of concern. He'd seen an excuse to make a move on her, more like. Rory Silverman had a reputation for chasing and bedding good-looking women. Obviously, he saw her as an easy target. The Conway girl on her own, miles from anywhere.

'Yes, my phone *is* out of order,' she conceded. 'I don't suppose you happened to report it for me?'

'Uh…no. I didn't think. Sorry. I was just thinking of *you*.'

Oh, sure, she thought, unable to see Rory Silverman as the gallant knight-to-the-rescue type. From what she knew of him, he didn't have a caring, heroic bone in his svelte body! He was just out for what he could get. A *woman*. The richer and more glamorous the better.

Not that he'd find any glamour *here* today. Far from it.

'You look different.' Rory ran expert eyes over her, apparently not caring that he was keeping her standing in puddles of water, with rain dripping from her umbrella onto her shoulders. His gaze lingered a second or two on the curves revealed by her white T-shirt, before flicking back to her face. His brow puckered. 'You look younger. Or something.'

Her mouth twitched. 'I guess you've only seen me in my glad rags, with all the warpaint on.'

He looked startled for a second, as if he'd never thought of her in terms of warpaint. 'You're still gorgeous, even without make-up,' he assured her, recovering his aplomb. 'With those lovely dark eyes of yours and that stunning black hair...' But it was obvious he preferred her all dolled up and dressed to kill, with her hair flowing loose over her shoulders, rather than tied back in a girlish ponytail.

'Er...' his gaze veered to the Land Cruiser '...just on your way out, are you?' He squinted through the drizzle at the blurred windscreen and the male shape behind, as if trying to see who was with her.

'I'm—' She stopped. She'd been about to tell him she was just running a neighbour home, but caught back the words in time. If Rory knew that, he might insist on driving on to Fernlea and waiting there until she came back.

If it had been anyone other than Rory Silverman, she would have welcomed some friendly, amenable company to come home to, after putting up with Mike O'Malley's cynical gibes and patronising taunts. But she certainly didn't want to come home to Rory Silverman. She wouldn't enjoy his company, for one thing, and she wouldn't be able to trust him to take no for an answer. Or to go home when she asked him to.

'Yes, afraid so...sorry.' She gave a shrug of her shoulders. She didn't want to sound *too* regretful and encourage him to try another time. 'You've come all this way in the rain for nothing. Your lovely car will be a mess.'

He winced. 'Never mind,' he muttered, 'a car wash will fix it.'

If she'd told him the truth about Mike and asked him to wait for her at Fernlea, his answer might have been different. Something smoother, along the lines of, Never mind, you're worth it. But she hadn't, and he was plainly anxious now to be on his way. With as little wear and tear to his precious car—his plaything, his status symbol—as possible.

'Look...um...' She glanced round to make sure Mike O'Malley wasn't advancing on her to blow sky-high her story about being on her way out with him. 'Why don't you drive on to Fernlea, Rory, and turn around there? It'll be too dangerous trying to turn around here on this narrow road. You don't want your nice car to get bogged.' Having to help him out of the mud would be the last straw. It was getting late enough already.

'I sure don't,' Rory said emphatically. 'OK, I will...thanks.'

'I think there's just room for you to get safely past the Land Cruiser,' she told him. 'You go ahead... I'll wait till you've gone past.' *If Mike thinks Rory's going to Fernlea to wait for me,* she thought, *let him. If he thinks I've invited Rory to stay the night, let him think that too. He'll think the worst of me anyway.*

'Right.' Rory nosed the Porsche forward, snaking his head round as he crawled past the big four-wheel drive to take a peek at her passenger. As Taryn sprinted back to the Land Cruiser with water squelching in her shoes, she saw Mike give a facetious wave.

Rory ignored it, or pretended not to notice. He wouldn't relish being cast aside for another man. That mocking wave would only rub it in.

'Sorry about that, Mike,' she said airily as she closed her dripping umbrella and tossed it into the back of the vehicle, before hauling herself up into the driver's seat. It was the first time, she realised, that she'd called him Mike. The name had come surprisingly easily to her lips.

She revved the engine. 'We'd better get a move on.' Chatting to Rory had wasted precious daylight.

'I can understand your anxiety to dispose of me and rush back home,' Mike drawled. 'A red Porsche is some bait... You're sure you still want to drive me all the way home?'

She felt a twinge of something like disappointment, mingled with irritation. So he did think Rory was going to Fernlea to wait for her. Well, of course...he would! Her mouth tightened. He would always think the worst of her.

'What choice do I have?' she growled. Mike O'Malley could think what he liked. She didn't care. If he wanted to believe that she was encouraging Rory Silverman, she wasn't going to tell him otherwise. Why should she? He wouldn't believe her anyway.

'You could always make me walk.'

'Oh, sure.' She hunched over the wheel, her tone fractious. 'Just let me concentrate, will you?'

They didn't talk after that, and she reached the bitumen road at the bridge without further mishap. Instead of turning right as she normally would, she swung the Land Cruiser round to the left, in the direction of the O'Malleys' property, knowing she had to pass a couple of other farms first.

The rain had eased at last to a light drizzle, and the

road they were on now was wider and in better condition, making progress quicker and easier.

'Pity you haven't built your new bridge yet between Fernlea and Plane Tree Flats,' Mike said after a while, a hint of steel in his voice at the mention of the property the O'Malleys had once owned and had wanted to buy back—until her father had supposedly snatched it from under their noses. 'We could have taken a short cut through Henderson's old farm and saved driving all this way round.'

'It's no trouble,' she said, her own tone brittle as she wondered what kind of reception she could expect from his father—if Patrick O'Malley happened to be around when she dropped off his son.

She was tempted to drop Mike off at the gate leading into the O'Malley property when they reached it, but it was still drizzling and it seemed a bit petty, with his house still some distance away...and up a steepish climb.

And Mike had instructions for her anyway.

'If you'll drive right up to the house,' he directed, 'I'll check our phone before you go home. If ours is OK, I'll ring up and report yours for you.'

She flicked him a faint look of surprise, oddly touched that he'd remembered...and would bother about her problems. 'Thanks. And what if yours is dead too?'

'If it is, maybe you could ask your Porsche-driving friend to report the problem for both of us...when he goes home. Assuming he's going back home tonight?'

She sucked in her breath. He was fishing. She had a feeling that whatever answer she gave he would manage to twist it around somehow—or at least make some cynical gibe about the company she kept. Well, let him fish. She wasn't biting.

'Let's just see if your phone's working.' It was a husky growl. 'They might have fixed the line by now.'

'Anything's possible.' She heard the cold edge to his voice and almost wished, contrarily, that she'd told him the truth…that she hadn't even asked Rory to wait for her, let alone to spend the night with her.

But why should she tell him? she thought in the next breath, remembering how Mike O'Malley despised her, simply because her family had money and spoke with a bit of a 'twang', and because they'd bought some land his father had wanted. It was none of his damned business!

'Stop here for a sec,' Mike said abruptly as they reached the milking sheds. 'I'll just let my father know I'm back.'

She tensed. *His father…the man who despised the Conways most of all.* 'I really don't want to hang around,' she muttered peevishly. 'It's starting to get dark.'

'I know… That's why I need to see him. To tell him I intend to follow you back in the ute…just to make sure you get back in one piece.'

Her eyes widened. 'Don't be silly, that's not necess—' She stopped, her eyes narrowing. 'You sure you don't just want to check up on who I might be entertaining for the evening? Or the *night*?'

That would be more like it, she thought. Michael O'Malley wanting to gather more ammunition to throw at her.

He gave a snort of laughter. Harsh, derisive laughter. 'If that's what you prefer to think, be my guest.' She flinched at the ice-cold edge to his voice. 'And if that's the type you go for, good luck to you.'

He threw open his door as he spoke, and jumped down, leaving her fuming. *He's not,* she wanted to shout after him, but she didn't. What was the point? He'd made up his mind about her.

'Michael!' A different voice rang out. She saw a man

approaching from the yards. He was tall, lean-hipped and wide-shouldered like his son, with a tough weathered face and a thatch of almost-white hair. 'So you're back, are you? Where's Caesar?' His eyes, Taryn suspected, would be the same piercing aqua as his son's, though it was hard to tell in the dimness.

'Hi, Dad. I'm afraid Caesar bolted in the storm and left me to—'

'No! It *can't* be!' Patrick O'Malley's voice sliced over his son. 'Not *you*!' He was staring up at the driver's side of the Land Cruiser now. Staring up at *her*. He took a step closer, his face twisting in fury and disbelief, causing Taryn's fingers to tighten on the wheel, her heart pounding.

Did Patrick O'Malley hate the Conways *that* much? she wondered shakily, flicking her tongue over her lips. And how had Mike's father recognised her? She'd never even met the man! Patrick O'Malley had refused to have anything to do with the Conways.

'*Crystal!*' he spat out, his eyes glinting slits in his leathery brown face. They were his son's eyes all right. 'I don't believe it! What in hell's name are *you*—?' He stopped, clamping his mouth shut, as if realising he'd made a monstrous mistake.

He stepped back, his eyes snapping to his son. 'Sorry, Michael. For a minute there I thought—' He shrugged, and jutted his jaw. 'Stupid mistake. The dim light played tricks on me. Of course it wouldn't be Crystal.'

Crystal? Taryn released the breath she'd been holding. *Who was Crystal?*

CHAPTER FOUR

'NOT to worry, Dad.' His son's profile, in the gathering dusk, was stony. 'There is a slight resemblance... I'll grant you that.'

Taryn shivered, Mike's steely tone cutting through her, numbing her. A resemblance? A resemblance to a girl called Crystal, who, apparently, wasn't wanted here. She swallowed, remembering Mike's cynical words to her, up in the forest.

'I knew it was too good to be true. A fairy-tale beauty with raven hair and stunning black eyes...'

Had the mysterious Crystal had raven hair and stunning black eyes too? Was he irresistibly drawn to raven-haired, dark-eyed females, she wondered dazedly, the way some men went for blondes?

The initial attraction, in her case, had soon evaporated, she recalled with a faint tremor. 'The girl of my dreams would never be a pampered city socialite...'

Had Crystal been a pampered city socialite?

Crystal... She drew in her lips, remembering the way Mike had mocked her about her name. 'I might have known it wouldn't be Jane or Mary.' She inhaled deeply. Crystal...Taryn...both unusual names...both dark-eyed brunettes...both from privileged backgrounds...

Was that it?

Had Mike O'Malley been emotionally involved with Crystal at some time? Had Crystal spurned him? Cheated on him? *Stolen* from him? *Something* must have happened between them to make the girl so unwelcome here...and to give Mike that huge chip on his shoulder, that cynical view of women from pampered, affluent backgrounds.

It would certainly explain a lot.

Mike was explaining *her* away now, to his father. 'Our neighbour—Miss Conway—offered me a lift home, Dad. We were both out riding when the storm hit.' His father barely glanced her way, his brow seeming to darken in the fading light.

'So you haven't seen Caesar, Dad?' Mike pressed. Switching the conversation away from her? 'He would have come home the back way.'

'No, I haven't seen him. I've been milking cows and keeping out of that damned rain.' The answer was curt. The word Conway, not Caesar, had brought that harshness to his voice, Taryn suspected. 'Smudge has just gone back to the yards to fetch something. He might know.'

'So you don't know if our phone's working or not?'

'No, I don't. Why? You need to call someone?' Irritation roughened his father's voice. He didn't know and he didn't care. He was anxious to get back to his cows.

Anxious to get away from the Conway girl, Taryn guessed, with a sigh. He hadn't even bothered to acknowledge her.

'No... I just want to check it,' Mike said. 'I'll check on Caesar too, then I'll be taking the ute out for a while. Won't be long.'

His father glanced sharply at him, but didn't ask any questions. I bet he'll have some later, though, Taryn thought with a hidden grimace.

'See you.' Patrick O'Malley raised a hand—perhaps meant to include her too—and stomped off.

Mike hauled himself back into the passenger's seat. 'Sorry about the delay.' Not sorry about his father's curtness, she noted. 'Just drive round to the yard behind the house, would you? If Caesar's back, he'll be there. Hopefully.'

'And if he isn't?'

'I'll worry about that if and when I need to.' He sounded a bit touchy himself, Taryn noticed. Was it the mention of Crystal?

They were passing his house now, heading for the gate leading round to the yards. Unlike Fernlea, which was set in an extensive old English garden among huge oaks, elms, golden ashes and cypress trees, the O'Malleys' sprawling weatherboard farmhouse had a garden of mostly native shrubs and trees, bordered by a privet hedge with a rose-covered arch over the front gate. There was a separate iron-roofed bungalow to one side of the house.

A charming, homely, comfortable-looking place, Taryn thought, but she made no comment, afraid that her passenger might think she was being patronising. Or false.

She swung the Land Cruiser into the gravel yard, pulling up where Mike indicated, close to a big open shed housing machinery and farm equipment. As he threw open his door and jumped out, a shape materialised out of the gloom, the headlights picking up a shortish, stocky young man with a shock of pale sandy hair. He had a roll of wire over his shoulder.

It was Smudge. She'd seen him a few times in the distance, and had heard about him now and then from Abby and Dino, the young couple working for her father.

'Ah, Mike...it's you.' Smudge greeted Mike in a broad Australian accent. 'I found Caesar in the yard. Ran off, did he?' He gave a grin.

'Left me for dead,' Mike said dryly. 'Is he all right?'

'Soaked, but seems OK. He's had a feed and he's back in his paddock now...under shelter.'

'Thanks, Smudge. Don't suppose you happen to know if our phone's working?'

'Huh?' Smudge shrugged. 'Dunno. Haven't been in the house. Look, I gotta fly. Patrick wants this wire.'

'Right. See you.'

As Smudge scuttled off, Mike came round to the driver's side and swung open her door.

'You'd better come in with me, Taryn, so we can report your phone...assuming ours is OK. It'll give you a chance to stretch your legs before you head back.'

She nodded. Her throat felt strangely dry. He was calling her Taryn now...not Miss Conway. But then, she'd called him Mike, so it was no big deal. It didn't mean he thought any more highly of her.

Her mind wasn't on what she was doing as she swung herself out of her seat. She missed her footing and might have tumbled into the puddles below if Mike hadn't been there to catch her.

She felt his hands gripping her waist. Firm, strong, protective hands... The hands, she thought tumultuously, of a man a woman could rely on to keep her safe.

Hands that could make a woman feel deliciously weak and breathlessly, bone-numbingly feminine.

For a ridiculous second she didn't want to move, didn't want to lose that dynamic strength, that rock-solid support. A support that made her tremble, deep inside.

Her eyelashes fluttered upwards. Their eyes met, black clashing with glittering turquoise.

She'd heard the saying 'time stood still' a million times, and had scorned it. But as his gaze swallowed hers, his face breathtakingly close, time *did* stand still. Time—everything around them—ceased to exist, caught in breathless suspension.

Her lips parted involuntarily. She wanted him to kiss her, she realised. If he tried to kiss her, she knew she wouldn't turn away. In that heady, endless second, she *longed* for him to kiss her...ached to feel his lips again, as she had up in the forest...to feel their supple warmth on hers...to experience again the dreamy, erotic sensations she'd felt when he'd kissed her before.

The brush of his lips on hers was there and gone before she could even react to it.

'Temptress,' he muttered, so softly that she barely heard the word. But she heard the underlying cynicism...or bitterness...or mistrust that came with it. Whatever it was, it jolted her back to earth.

'I'm OK...you can let me go now,' she bit out, drawing back. As his hands dropped away, she mumbled, 'I'm not usually that clumsy...thanks.'

'Let's go in.' He turned on his heel, the roughness in his voice bringing a flush of humiliation to her cheeks as she followed him into his father's surprisingly modern, streamlined kitchen. Did he think she'd been deliberately tempting him? *Because she was that kind of girl? A rich, spoilt, fun-seeking playgirl?*

Was that how he saw her?

A trembling sigh slipped from her. He believed she'd asked Rory Silverman to wait for her...to spend the night with her. What else could he think?

Mike snatched up the phone and pressed it to his ear. 'Normal dial tone,' he reported, his tone still terse. He dialled a number, and waited. 'I want to report a phone out of order. Just a minute...' He thrust the phone at her. 'They want your phone number and address.'

While she was giving the details, she saw him move over to a huge refrigerator-freezer and pull out a bottle of lemonade. Not beer, she noticed. Was he avoiding alcohol because they'd both be driving back to Fernlea?

Did that mean he still intended to follow her in the ute?

'Oh... I see,' she said into the phone. 'Good. Thank you.'

Mike raised an enquiring eyebrow as she hung up.

'Someone's already reported it,' she said. 'All the farms on our side of the river are cut off. There was a land slip, apparently, due to the rain, and the underground cables were affected. They're sending someone to fix it. I'd better be off,' she said, grimacing at the breathlessness in her voice.

'You won't have a glass of lemonade first? Or something else?' He dashed some lemonade into one glass and let the bottle hover over another.

'No, thanks. You stay and have yours. I'll just—'

'I'm coming too.' He scooped up the filled glass and tossed down the contents in a couple of swallows. 'You were good enough to drive me home. The least I can do is see you safely back to your place. To make sure you get there.'

'I think I'm capable of getting back in one piece,' she protested, even as something inside her jumped at what seemed a case of old-fashioned gallantry...a rare phenomenon in this day and age, which a girl didn't often encounter. Certainly not without strings attached.

But maybe he simply wanted to square things between them, so that he didn't need to feel in her debt. Mike O'Malley didn't strike her as a man who'd want to feel beholden to anyone. Least of all a Conway.

'If you ran off the road or hit something and there was no one around to help you,' he persisted, 'think how I'd feel.' His voice was gruff. 'I'd feel it was my fault for dragging you out in this stinking weather. It'll be even more dangerous now that it's dark.'

Her eyes wavered. 'Think how I'd feel', he'd said. But he wasn't saying he'd be *worried* about her...just that he'd blame himself if anything happened to her. Was he afraid that someone—her father, perhaps—might hold him responsible if something nasty did happen to her?

She almost laughed aloud at the thought of Mike O'Malley being afraid of anything, let alone her father, a man he despised. Mike was his own man…tough, self-assured and confident…a man who wouldn't bow or quake before anyone.

Whatever his motivation was, he wouldn't be thinking of *her*. She could tell by the roughness in his voice that feelings or kindness didn't come into it. No…he just wanted to wipe the slate clean so he wouldn't have to feel he owed her anything.

'Well, follow me, then, if you insist.' She knew she sounded ungracious but she couldn't help it. Were there no men with purely gallant, selfless motives any more? 'I'd hate your conscience to bother you if I didn't get home in one piece.'

As he nodded curtly and waved her ahead of him out of the house, she commented in a milder tone, feeling a rush of shame at her lack of gratitude, 'Nice kitchen. Spotlessly clean and tidy for an all-male household. Who deserves the credit? You…Smudge…or your father?'

She was fishing, she realised, to find out if Mike was living at home again…or just passing through. She hadn't asked him outright. She hadn't wanted him to think…

She swallowed. To think what? That she cared if he stayed or went? She didn't care! Of course she didn't. They were poles apart…as alienated as the Hatfields and McCoys…as the Montagues and Capulets…and they always would be. Mike O'Malley would make sure of that.

'None of us can take the credit really,' he lazily admitted, 'although we're all quite handy when we need to be. My father's just had a new kitchen put in. And we have a local girl who comes over twice a week from Hallston to do the cleaning, cooking, or whatever's required. A farmer's daughter. Lovely girl. Hard-working,

sweet-tempered, down-to-earth. Pretty too. Very pretty.'
He winked as he followed her out.

She felt a stab of...what? Envy? Jealousy? She
scoffed at the notion. She'd never been jealous in her
life, and he was the last man...

She compressed her lips at the very idea. If she felt
anything it was pique, because he was obviously having
another sly dig at *her*. He would never describe the pampered Conway girl as hard-working, sweet-tempered and
down-to-earth. Or pretty either, for that matter. Her looks
only reminded him of Crystal, her apparent look-
alike...the girl who'd seemingly hurt him...or who'd
done *something* to turn the O'Malley men against her.

Had the poor creature deserved such vitriol and rejec-
tion...or not?

When she reached the Land Cruiser she made one last
attempt to dissuade him from following her. 'I really
don't need an escort. I'm a big girl now.'

'I'm sure your Porsche-driving friend would agree
with you.'

Her eyes narrowed in quick suspicion. Was that the
real reason he wanted to escort her home? To see if Rory
had stayed? To confirm his low opinion of her? It would
be well into the night by the time they got back. If Rory
had stayed, he'd be unlikely to leave until morning!

Rebellion stirred in her heart. Who did Mike
O'Malley think he was? Her moral guardian? Her private
life was none of his business!

Let him follow her home, she decided mutinously.
She would even pretend that Rory *had* stayed...that she
couldn't wait to get home to her waiting Romeo.

One thing she was resolved never to reveal to Michael
O'Malley: that he, or anything he did or said, could affect her in any way whatsoever!

'We'd better hurry then,' she ground out, 'before he
gives up waiting for me.'

'Oh, I'm sure he'll think you're well worth waiting for,' came the silky response.

She slid behind the wheel and slammed the door.

Although it was completely dark by now, the rain, mercifully, had finally stopped altogether and the heavy clouds had drifted away to reveal a rising half-moon. The drive home was uneventful, although she was conscious all the way of Mike's headlights behind her.

She swung into Fernlea's driveway and pulled up in the cobble-stoned yard, slewing the Land Cruiser round to block Mike's view of the darkened double garage further on, where Rory's car might or might not be lurking under shelter, next to her Ford Laser.

As she jumped out, she saw O'Malley wave a hand as he swung the ute round. Something caught in her throat. Wasn't he even going to stop and say goodnight?

'Wait!' she shrieked, running up to him, forcing him to bring the ute to a halt. 'I just wanted to say…thanks,' she said lamely as he poked his head out of the side window.

'No need. We're even now…quits. One good turn deserves another, so they say.' He gave a brief half-smile that deepened the lines round his mouth. The moonlight was casting shadows, and she couldn't be sure if his eyes were smiling too… Probably not.

'We're even now…quits.'

So that *was* why he'd followed her home…so that he wouldn't have to feel indebted to her. She sighed. No…an O'Malley would never want that. To be indebted to a Conway.

'Your friend seems to have gone,' O'Malley murmured. Then, after a pause, 'Are you disappointed? I'm sure you must be…just a little. Missing out on a torrid night of fun and frolic with the polo world's most eligible bachelor.'

She glared at him. So he'd recognised Rory

Silverman... Mike O'Malley didn't miss much. He might try to make out that he was a simple, down-to-earth dairy farmer's son, but he was also a well-educated, highly qualified chemical engineer and a qualified vet...and, from what she'd heard from the neighbours, a smart, well-travelled, ambitious go-getter along with it.

So he thought she had designs on Rory Silverman, did he? He thought she was disappointed that Rory hadn't waited for her? 'A torrid night of fun and frolic', indeed! She curled her lip in swift resolve. Well, let him think that fun and frolic was precisely what she *was* going to have!

'I told Rory to park his car in the garage, out of the rain.' Her eyes taunted him in the wash of the moonlight. 'I'd better go in...he's waited quite long enough, don't you think? Still, I guess he must think I'm worth it...as you said.'

The gaze that fastened on hers held a dark glitter. Of derision? Distaste? Disappointment? Something dipped inside her.

'Um...by the way...' She hesitated, biting her lip. But the need to know was too strong. 'Are you back home for good this time? Or just here for a short visit?'

She gulped as the questions leapt out. Did she want to hear that he was back home for good...or not? She dreaded the prospect of having such a hostile neighbour—a man who openly despised everything about her—and yet...

He was also the most intriguing, most challenging, most vibrantly exciting man she'd ever met, ever pitted her mettle against. And the sexiest. Her heartbeat quickened as she waited for his answer.

'I'm afraid it's just a short visit,' he told her, and her heart plummeted in a way she hadn't expected. 'I've just come home to spend a few days with my father and to

attend a Rotary dinner in Korumburra tomorrow night.
I'm leaving at the end of the week for America…'

America? In a few *days*? Her mind reeled. Not the
backblocks of Australia this time, but *America*. Half a
world away.

'I'll be touring the States, promoting my new chemical device,' he explained without going into details,
obviously thinking it would be beyond her comprehen-
sion—or of no interest to her. 'I'll be working on a few
other things at the same time, before moving on to
Europe…to Holland in particular. I'll be away for about
twelve to eighteen months…maybe longer.'

Her breath stopped. A *year*? Maybe more?

She should have cheered…felt a rush of relief, of wild
elation. This man had nothing but contempt for her and
her family. He'd done nothing but taunt and criticise her
from the moment they'd met. So why did she feel
so…so bereft, as if a light had gone out in her life…as
if a lead weight had settled in her stomach?

She needed her head read! The last thing she needed
in her life right now was a man interfering with her
plans, getting under her skin, invading her thoughts…
and, worse, spoiling her concentration. She had to focus
all her mind and emotion and energy on her riding…on
reaching her goal…on winning a place in the Sydney
Olympic team…not spend her time sparring with a man
who despised her…or mooning over him, for heaven's
sake. The sooner he went the better!

'Well, I wish you well,' she said, striving at a coolness
that until today had always come so easily to her. 'I'm
sure your father will miss you.' *I certainly won't,* she
vowed. *I won't.*

'My father's all for it,' Mike O'Malley assured her, a
faint tartness in his tone, as if he suspected she was
having a snide crack at him for going off and leaving
his father in the lurch again.

'Well...good for you.' She shrugged, wondering if she could believe it. Or was Patrick O'Malley getting used to his son's long absences?

'I wish you well too, Taryn, with the Olympics,' Mike said, but the bantering note was back, rather spoiling it. It was plain he didn't take her lofty ambition seriously, didn't think *she* was serious. 'I'll watch out for your name when the Olympic equestrian team's announced.'

And then he spoilt it even more. 'And good luck with your flashy polo player too...an old school acquaintance of mine, incidentally.' But obviously not a *friend*. 'I'm sure your parents will be ecstatic if you manage to land him.'

She bit back the savage retort on her lips. Let him think what he liked. He would, no matter what she told him.

'Plenty of fish in the sea if I don't!' she snapped instead.

'Quite so. Bigger fish too,' he purred with an infuriatingly sardonic smile. 'You can do better than Rory Silverman, I'm sure...if you put your mind to it. Especially if you become an Olympic gold medallist. The world will be at your feet then. The sleeping beauty could end up with a *real* prince.'

She clenched her hands into white-knuckled fists, her chest heaving under her white T-shirt. The prospect of being an Olympic champion one day had always excited her...spurred her on...buoyed her through the tough times. But Mike O'Malley's cynicism—his scathing opinion of her—had taken some of the gloss off her dream...tarnishing it, turning it into something ugly and calculating. Or a spoilt rich girl's whim.

'I'm glad you're not going to be a neighbour of mine, Michael O'Malley,' she heard herself biting back, flailing him with her eyes. 'And I hope that when you do come back—*if* you come back—you'll decide to live a long, long way from here!'

'Oh, dear.' His eyes mocked her. 'You'd banish me from my father's reach for ever? Your concern for him appears to have been sadly short-lived!'

Heat prickled her cheeks. 'Good*night*, Mr O'Malley!' she grated, twisting away. Now she couldn't wait to get away from him. 'I have someone waiting,' she reminded him, wishing with all her heart that she had. Someone who would make her forget Michael O'Malley and everything about him.

'Well, good luck,' he said, his tone heavily ironic. 'And thank you for confirming what I've long suspected. That beautiful dream-girls don't exist.'

He paused, his teeth showing in a tigerish smile. 'But what the hell? I've an urge for a night of passion myself...and I know just the old flame who'll give it to me. Goodnight, Miss Conway. Perhaps we'll lock horns again before I leave.'

'That's most unlikely!' she bit back. She was trembling as the ute roared off. Hot, angry tears blurred her eyes. 'Good riddance, Michael O'Malley,' she breathed. 'And thank *you* too...for showing *me* that dream princes don't exist either!'

Around lunchtime three days later Rory Silverman paid her an unexpected visit. She was busy in the stables, but his opening sally made her hand freeze on the saddle she was cleaning.

'Was Mike O'Malley the man you were with the other night?' he asked, looking smug.

Her eyes narrowed. 'Maybe. Why do you ask?'

'I thought I recognised him.' He leaned against the tackroom wall. 'I met his ex-fiancée Crystal at a Rotary dinner in Korumburra a couple of nights ago...'

Crystal... The name jolted through her. So the mysterious Crystal had been Mike O'Malley's *fiancée* once…a woman he'd loved deeply enough to want to marry. A woman who'd later hurt him or let him down in some way…and who apparently resembled *her*.

'We've known each other all our lives, Crystal and I,' Rory purred. 'We're first cousins. She was home for her father's sixtieth birthday and she came along to the Rotary dinner with him. My parents and I joined them.'

Crystal had been at the same Rotary dinner that *Mike* had gone to… Taryn's heart wobbled. Had they met up again that night?

She bowed her head over the saddle and began to rub vigorously with the damp sponge.

'Rory, you'll have to excuse me… I've a lot to do,' she growled. 'I'm competing in a show-jumping competition at the weekend.'

'I can't stay anyway.' Rory gave a lazy shrug. 'But there's something you should know, Taryn…for your own protection.'

She glanced up, frowning. 'What are you talking about?'

'Your friend Mike O'Malley and his ex-fiancée Crystal,' Rory confided with a pitying smile, 'spent the night together. I saw Crystal the next day and she told me. We've always been like brother and sister…we've no secrets from each other. She said they met up after the dinner and…it just happened. They just lost control.'

Taryn's hand faltered on the saddle. Her head was spinning. Was it true?

Mike's wolfish words leapt back. 'I've an urge for a night of passion myself…and I know just the old flame who'll give it to me.'

She gripped the saddle to steady herself.

'Of course, Crystal's a married woman now, but when the cat's away,' Rory murmured with a wicked leer, 'well, can you blame them for wanting a bit of a fling for old times' sake? They're two red-blooded adults and they were in love once. Obviously still can't resist each other...despite their break-up a year or so ago.'

Taryn tried valiantly to stay calm, to appear indifferent, but her mind was still reeling. Mike had *slept* with Crystal? *A married woman?*

Her mouth twisted. Whatever Crystal had done to him in the past, however much she'd hurt him, it was obvious that his passion for his ex-fiancée had overridden his hurt feelings. And any morals he might have possessed.

'Not that anything can come of it, with Crystal married now.' Rory gave a shrug. 'She's already gone back to her tycoon husband in New Zealand.' He paused, as if trying to read her carefully masked expression. 'I dare say Mike's already kicking himself for letting his feelings flare out of control...the poor fool never could resist her. Their break-up really knocked him for six, you know. I guess by now he's feeling hurt and used all over again. And disgusted with himself for being so weak.'

Not as disgusted as I feel, Taryn thought shakily. After all Mike's bitter talk of dream-girls not existing, he'd rushed straight into the arms of his original dream-girl...the woman who'd made him so cynical in the first place.

'I hope you weren't too keen on him, Taryn.' Rory couldn't hide the gloating light in his pearl-grey eyes.

'Of course not.' Was that pathetic croak her own voice? 'I barely knew him.' Then why did she feel as if she were disintegrating? Why did she feel so sick?

'That's good, because Mike left for America this morning.'

He'd gone already? Without even saying goodbye? Despite her revulsion at what Mike had done, she felt a knife-stab of hurt...until icy common sense reasserted itself. It was just as well he *had* gone. If he'd turned up now, she would have spat in his face!

Her shoulders slumped in relief when Rory drove off. One more glance at his gloating face and she would have spat at *him*! She let out a quivering sigh. She ought to be grateful to Rory. He'd just confirmed all over again what she already knew. That dream princes didn't exist!

Well, you live and learn, she thought bitterly, squeezing the sponge as tightly as she could and wishing it were Mike O'Malley's neck. 'I'm *glad* you've gone, Michael O'Malley. *Glad!*'

It was fourteen months before she saw him again, and by then her life had changed irrevocably...calamitously. She'd lost the person dearest to her...her greatest champion...and her dream of Olympic glory had been shattered for all time.

Along with a part of herself...

CHAPTER FIVE

TARYN was about to step into her Ford Laser at the hospital car park in Warragul when a grey Range Rover eased into the vacant spot next to hers. She flicked a glance at the driver behind the wheel, then looked again, her body jolting in shock.

Was it...? Could it be...?

Of course it was him. She'd been half expecting him back ever since she'd heard about his father's heart attack. Patrick O'Malley himself had told her, only a few minutes ago, that his young farmhand Smudge had contacted his son in Holland to let him know.

But she hadn't really believed that Mike would come home so soon...so quickly. Or even come at all. His father was already recovering and clamouring to go home—his heart attack hadn't been as serious as first thought—and Smudge was quite capable of taking charge of the dairy farm until Patrick was fit enough to take over.

'Smudge should never have worried my son about me,' Patrick had grumbled to her from his hospital bed. 'Now that I'm getting better, there's no need for Mike to come home. I've told Smudge to tell him that. Mike's only just started his stint in Holland.'

But he *had* come home. And now, she realised as she stood with her fingers frozen on her car keys, he was looking at *her*...in much the same stunned way.

'Well, Miss Conway,' he hailed her as he threw open his door and unfolded his impressive frame to its six-foot-plus height. 'Fancy seeing you here. You're visiting someone too?'

She felt a tingling in her legs as he stepped over to join her. She'd forgotten how tall he was—she had to tilt her chin and squint up at him in the bright February sun—forgotten how startlingly good-looking he was, with those piercing blue-green eyes, that healthily sun-bronzed skin. The vivid, bittersweet dreams she'd once had of him had faded over the past traumatic months, blurring his image.

He was wearing a buff-coloured sports shirt, pale drill trousers and tan shoes. Quite a change from his usual boots, faded jeans and bush shirt. He'd obviously come straight from the airport.

'I…was visiting your father,' she admitted tentatively, wondering if he'd be upset that she—a Conway—had been to see his father before he'd had a chance to. 'I was sorry to hear about his heart attack.' She couldn't meet him in the eye. Discomfiting memories were stirring, bringing a wariness that hooded her gaze. 'But they say he's coming along fine.'

'Good of you to visit him.' She could feel Mike's eyes searching her face, making her wish she'd checked her hair and lipstick, and worn something a little less daggy than a loose shirt and jeans. Not that he hadn't seen her looking even worse, the only other time they'd been together. He'd seen her soaked to the skin and scrubbed bare of make-up altogether.

'I didn't know you and my father were on speaking terms…'

They hadn't been…until today. But, having heard about Patrick's heart attack on the neighbourhood grapevine, she'd decided it was time to forget their differences and offer an olive branch. The Conway-O'Malley feud had been going on for far too long.

'We're close neighbours.' She shrugged. 'It worried me that there was antagonism between us.' Her eyes were cool, evasive, letting Mike know that he wasn't necessarily included in the reconciliation.

'Well, I'm glad you've broken the ice...' Mike seemed to hesitate, his own eyes appearing to soften. 'Smudge told me about your accident, Taryn. He heard about it from the young couple working for you.' He touched her arm, ever so lightly. She jumped at the brief contact and stepped back. 'I'm sorry about your father, Taryn. That was tough for you...mighty tough. I know how close you were to him.'

She moistened her lips with a flick of her tongue, wondering if his sympathy was genuine. After the snide comments he'd made about Hugh Conway in the past, it didn't seem likely. Not that she wanted his sympathy...she'd had enough sympathy to last a lifetime. Not that she wanted *anything* from Mike O'Malley. Not after...

She swallowed, closing her heart against his charm.

'Thank you,' she said tightly. 'Yes...I miss him.' She missed him terribly. Her father had always encouraged her dreams and ambitions, had always lent a sympathetic ear, had always understood her passion for horses and the outdoor life. Far more than her mother ever had.

'Smudge told me that *you* were in hospital too for a while, back in Melbourne...' Mike paused, frowning slightly as her eyes flickered under his. 'Are you completely recovered now?'

She drew in a quick breath as her mind conjured an image of twisted metal, of searing pain, of her father lying so still and pale beside her...and the shocked realisation that her foot was trapped...crushed...

She let out her breath. 'Yes, I'm fine, thanks. Completely recovered.' He mightn't think so when he saw her walking like a lame duck. Rory Silverman had been horrified when he'd come to visit her at Fernlea after returning from an overseas polo trip last month. She hadn't seen him since.

Mike peered into her face, as if doubting her offhand assertion. 'Smudge mentioned that you were no longer riding competitively...or so he'd heard. Is this just a temporary set-back?'

She frowned, mistrusting the concern in his eyes, in his voice. He'd never believed she'd been serious anyway—let alone Olympic gold material—so how could she believe that he cared now?

'No... I've given it away. For good.' She spoke carelessly, as if it didn't matter to her. She didn't want to talk about it. Mike O'Malley was here to visit his father, not to hear a sob story from *her*...which he'd be bound to think was simply an excuse for giving up on her one-time dream, after finding the going too hard.

And he'd be gone again soon...once he'd checked that his father was all right. He didn't *need* to know.

'Does this mean you'll be giving up Fernlea as well?' Mike asked. His eyes were unreadable now, his tone as careless as her own. 'When I spoke to Dad last, he mentioned that you'd been selling off your cattle and that you'd told the young couple working for you that you wouldn't be needing them for much longer.'

'You seem to have discussed me a lot with your father and your hired help,' she said, rather more sharply than she'd intended. *Why* had they discussed her? A part of her wanted to know, while another part—a more rational part—knew the answer. Because they'd wanted to find out if Fernlea was to be sold again...and were curious to know who their new neighbours might be.

Hoping, no doubt, they'd be *real* farmers this time, rather than part-time hobby farmers...rich city slickers...which the Conways *were*, as far as the O'Malleys were concerned.

Well, they'd know soon enough what she was planning to do. Mike's father already knew a small part of her plan...as of a few minutes ago.

She hadn't bothered Patrick with the rest of it...with her own personal plans for Fernlea. She'd been so alarmed when he'd suddenly closed his eyes and begun swallowing convulsively that she'd hastily summoned a nurse and quietly withdrawn from his room, hoping she hadn't triggered a relapse. She'd stayed around just long enough to ensure that he was all right. When the sister had come out of the ward with a bright smile and the assurance that her visit had done him the world of good, she'd left, sighing in relief.

Mike simply smiled at her snappish comment. 'I'm afraid I didn't hear about your accident, or about your father's death, Taryn, until some time after it happened. I've been moving around a fair bit. I know nothing about your own injuries, or how bad they were. All I know is that you came back to Fernlea to recuperate after you came out of hospital.'

She was about to correct him and say, Out of *rehab*— the hospital was much earlier—but she didn't, knowing it would only lead to further questions, and would delay him. She simply nodded instead.

'You *are* OK?' His eyes were searching hers again, as if he'd sensed that she wasn't telling him everything.

'I feel great,' she assured him, and she did. It could have been so much worse. She could have lost her foot altogether. Or her life...like her father had lost his. Instantly, thank heaven, without having to suffer. She turned away quickly, before Mike could see the tears that sprang to her eyes.

She gulped hard, and without turning back, muttered stiffly, 'Good to see you again, Mike,' and then swooped into her car.

'You too.'

Meaningless platitudes, she mused with a sigh as she drove off. She didn't expect to see him again.

Did she want to? Or care, one way or the other?

Damn it, she *did*. Seeing him again had shaken her. Her hands, she realised, were trembling on the wheel and her breath was ragged, quivering in her throat. Even her teeth were chattering, as if she were suffering from mild shock, or from the cold. Only it wasn't cold to-day…it was a perfect late-February summer's day, with the faintest breeze…a pleasant change after the oppressive heatwaves they'd been having lately.

The sight of her shaking hands made her tremble even more. Since the accident she'd been remarkably controlled, even appearing insensitive and unfeeling to some people. She'd passed each day like an automaton…showing a cool, calm, brave face to the world, and doing her mourning—for her father, for her lost dreams—in private, without ever allowing her grief to swamp her. Wondering sometimes if she still *had* feelings, or if they'd died along with everything else she'd lost.

But the way she felt now…

She hadn't felt like this in a long time. As if a part of her was still tremblingly alive, still awake to feelings, still able to be touched.

Still able to be hurt.

She heaved a deep, tremulous sigh. And Mike O'Malley, she had a feeling, was the one man—the only man she'd ever met—who was capable of touching her deeply enough to inflict that pain.

She threw herself into vigorous physical work when she arrived back at Fernlea. She had so much to do…so much still to work out to prepare for her exciting new venture. Dino and Abby had been helping her with her horses, now that the cattle had almost all been sold off and they had less to do. So far the young couple hadn't found another cattle farm to manage, and she'd told them they were welcome to stay until they did...if they were prepared to help her with the horses and with whatever work was needed to get her new set-up underway.

They'd agreed like a shot. The couple had been looking after the entire property for her since the accident, and they'd already come to know and care about her horses...the thoroughbred show-jumpers that just might have taken her to Olympic glory if fate hadn't intervened.

She was even considering offering Abby and Dino a new permanent position at Fernlea, if they were interested in a change from cattle farming to horse care and training...and were prepared to live above the stables, in the roomy loft she and her family had been using as a guest house since they'd restored it to its former glory...or rather, since converting it to clean, solid comfort.

The young couple couldn't go on living where they were for much longer, in the old house her father had put them in. Not now that she was selling off Plane Tree Flats...the fertile piece of land, with its hillside farmhouse, that had formerly belonged to Charley Henderson, and before that to the O'Malleys.

A smile touched her lips at the thought of the land coming full circle...

She realised the light was fading. The sun was already out of sight behind the hills. Abby and Dino would be heading off home shortly, back to Plane Tree Flats for the night. Why not ask them right now, before they finished up for the day? They needn't give their answer on the spot...they could go home and think about it overnight.

As for herself, she would have an early dinner and

spend the evening catching up on her reading and paperwork.

She was about to whip some eggs to make herself an omelette for dinner when she heard the sound of a car in the yard. She ambled over to the window and glanced out, but it was completely dark outside by now and there were no lights on in the yard. Just a pair of car headlights that died into darkness as the growling engine coughed into silence.

Was it Dino in the couple's battered old ute? Had he forgotten something? Or did he want to tell her they'd changed their minds about staying on, after earlier accepting her offer? They'd both agreed in a flash, which had surprised her. Maybe they'd had second thoughts and wanted more time to think about it.

She threw open the kitchen door, switched on the verandah lights—and the yard lights as well—and saw not Dino, but Mike O'Malley striding towards her.

Her mouth went dry and her breath quickened. 'Mike! I... You... ' Her hand fluttered in the air. She sounded impossibly, stupidly flustered. As she tried to pull herself together, he grinned.

'No shotgun? No poker? No branding iron? Just a— what *is* that in your hand? An egg flip? A strange weapon to fend off intruders in the night. Or did you know it was me?' His eyes glittered in the artificial light.

Her lip twitched, her tension easing. But only a trifle. 'Of course I didn't know it was you.' She was relieved that her voice sounded more normal now. 'I thought it was Dino...my—' She gulped, about to say 'my father's manager', but of course he wasn't that any more. 'The man who works for me.'

'Does he often visit you at night...without his wife?' Mike asked, and there was a sardonic note in his voice now that made her wonder if he genuinely believed that something might be going on between the 'lady of the manor' and her hired help. He'd never thought much of her, she recalled darkly. In Mike O'Malley's cynical eyes, she'd be the very type who'd relish playing around with another woman's husband.

She scowled. As if he could talk! A man who'd had an overnight fling with his ex-fiancée! A married woman!

'You're visiting me without *your* wife,' she retorted tartly. 'Unless you have her tucked away in your Range Rover?' she added sweetly, peering through the gloom at its shadowy outline. 'Assuming you've tied the knot since you've been away?'

Was it possible he'd finally stopped carrying a torch for the irresistible Crystal and married someone else? Or was he still a free man?

He gave a short laugh...a laugh with more derision than mirth. 'Marriage isn't high on my list of priorities. No... I'm here on my own. I suppose, after the crack I made a second ago, you're not going to invite me in?' His eyes glittered soulfully in the wash of the verandah light.

'I shouldn't,' she agreed, feeling inexplicably buoyed all of a sudden. Because he hadn't married anyone? Why should *that* buoy her? He'd be the last man in the world she'd ever want as a husband...even if marriage was on *her* agenda. She'd never be able to trust him!

And she'd be the last woman *he'd* ever want, if his cynical gibes in the past were anything to go by.

'Well...' She hesitated deliberately. 'A girl has to think of her reputation. Especially when she lives alone. And you *have* kindly reminded me of the dangers of entertaining male callers at night. I wouldn't want any-one to get the wrong idea. You know how people talk.' She glared meaningfully up into his face...and felt that odd tingling sensation all over again as her eyes clashed with his.

'OK, I take back what I said.' He held her gaze for a chaotic second. But the expression in the piercing blue eyes was unreadable. 'By the way, talking of entertaining male callers at night...how *is* Rory Silverman these days?'

She sucked in a fractious breath. He was reminding her that he wasn't the first man she'd entertained alone at night...or so he *thought*. She cursed under her breath. It was her own stupid fault that he thought her easy...fast...promiscuous. She'd let him think she'd invited Rory to stay that night. She'd *taunted* him about it.

She gasped as he caught her hand. 'Wh-what are you doing?'

'Checking for a ring. Or did the romance fizzle out?'

She snatched her hand back, his touch jolting her. 'Romance? Who said there was a romance?' Her voice was pathetically husky. 'Just because a man visited me one evening...'

'So...that was the last you saw of him...was it?'

'I didn't say that.' She was about to add, But I don't expect to see him again...nor would I want to, as she recalled Rory's sickened reaction at the sight of her lame foot. But she didn't want to tell Mike about that. She was damned if she was going to have him feeling sorry for her.

'No... I don't suppose you could,' Mike murmured.

She frowned. What did that cryptic remark mean? 'I'm too busy to see *anyone* at the moment,' she bit out. 'Men are a low priority in my life right now.' A tremor ran through her as she said it. How could she ever be sure if a man loved her for herself, gammy foot and all...or if he was after her for the small fortune—the investments and properties—that she'd inherited from her father?

Mike refrained from commenting. 'Look, can I come in or not?' He cocked his head at her, his dark hair—wild as ever—tumbling over his brow. 'Or do I have to speak to you out here on the doorstep? You can keep the door open and one finger on the phone if you don't feel safe.'

She smiled wanly. So he wanted to speak to her. Well, of course he did. Why else would he have come? He'd hardly be making a social call at this hour...just to *see* her again.

'I'm sure that won't be necessary,' she said testily. 'I survived once before when you came into the house while I was here on my own...if you remember.'

But I only just survived, she thought, turning pink as she recalled the towel draped low on his hips and the expanse of tanned muscular flesh on show. And why, for heaven's sake, had she asked him to *remember* it? She could have kicked herself.

She turned sharply, almost flouncing away as she led him inside, conscious that he was following, close behind. Conscious that he would now be aware of her limp. She wondered if he felt repulsed, like Rory Silverman... or sorry for her like so many of her friends. Or was he wondering if it was simply a temporary injury that would get better in time? He made no comment, leaving her none the wiser.

As she plonked the egg whisk down on the bench beside the bowl of eggs waiting to be whipped, she heard him pull the kitchen door shut behind him.

Without looking round, she asked edgily, wondering again what had brought him here, 'Would you like a drink?'

The hairs on her scalp lifted as he stepped up behind her and peered over her shoulder, his shadowed jaw almost brushing her heated cheek…causing her to wonder wildly how it would feel, scraping against her skin.

'You're just preparing your dinner?' he asked, spying the bowl of eggs. 'Look, don't let me hold you up.'

'Have you had yours?' she tossed back without thinking. As her heart fluttered at the thought of him staying to share a meal, she was mentally calculating how many eggs she would need to feed a man of Mike O'Malley's size and appetite.

'What, dinner? No, I'll have it when I get back.' He paused. 'Unless you're offering…'

She shrugged, trying to quell a host of churning butterflies inside. 'You'd be happy with an omelette?'

'Would I! I thought it was scrambled eggs…which would have been fine too,' he hastened to add. 'But an omelette…now that's *real* cooking. It requires finesse…a real knack…or it ends up scrambled eggs anyway.'

She laughed, a trifle unsteadily. 'Now you're making me nervous. I'm no cordon bleu cook. Take a seat while I find some more eggs. Then I'll get you to chop up some tomatoes, and some of my home-grown parsley. And maybe you'd like some bacon?' She hadn't intended to prepare and cook any filling for herself, but now that she was cooking for two…for a hungry, strapping man…

She even enjoyed cooking for him. And appreciated his help, chopping up the savoury filling. They both enjoyed the result, washing it down with some Chardonnay she'd been keeping in the fridge for unexpected visitors…never dreaming that her next visitor would be Mike O'Malley.

They were still in the kitchen, sitting either side of the solid old table in the centre of the room. She hadn't suggested going into the dining-room to eat, or even into the cosy den where she often ate meals herself, with a book propped in front of her. She still didn't know why he'd come, and she was wary of getting too cosy and comfortable with him.

Just as she was beginning to wonder if he had, after all, come simply to see her and spend some time with her, he showed that he hadn't.

CHAPTER SIX

'So...' HE sat back in his chair, his empty plate in front of him, his long fingers curled round the stem of his wineglass. 'You've decided to sell up.'

She stiffened. Was *that* why he'd come? Because he believed she was selling up? There was no discernible mockery or derision in his tone, no expression at all. The piercing eyes under the heavy brows were unreadable.

As her lips parted to set him straight, he asked smoothly, 'Decided to be a full-time city slicker again, have you? Horse-riding's lost its appeal, finally? Or did your injury force the decision on you?' His tone softened a little.

She swallowed. 'On the contrary...' Her bottom lip quivered even as her dark eyes flashed. She didn't want his pity. 'I'm more keen on horse-riding than ever. I'm just not competing any more.'

'So you're not selling your horses? Just the cattle...and Fernlea? Where will you keep your horses? You'll look for agistment closer to town?'

'I'll be keeping them *here*,' she told him with a toss of her head. 'Where did you get the idea I'm selling Fernlea? I'm not.'

That floored him. But only for a second. 'But you *are* selling off Plane Tree Flats...Henderson's old place? And your cattle?'

'That's right.'

'But you're keeping Fernlea...the land, the house, and your horses.' He spelt it out.

77

'Correct.' She eyed him sideways. 'Is that all right with you?'

His face relaxed in a quick grin. 'I didn't mean to give you the third degree. I just wanted to know what you were intending to do with Fernlea. I'd have made an offer for it myself if you'd been selling...we could have used the land to put in crops.'

Her heart dipped. So that was the only reason he was interested in what her plans were. The only reason he'd called in on her tonight.

'I'm sorry.' She spoke carelessly. Coolly. 'All I'm selling off is the piece of land across the river. Plane Tree Flats. And the old house that goes with it.'

Something glimmered in his eyes. 'And you've offered it to my father...for far less than *your* father paid for it.'

She shrugged. 'There's been a slump in property values since you went away. And I want a quick sale, without any hassles. Besides...the land originally belonged to the O'Malleys, so it seemed only right to offer it to your father first. Especially as I know he wanted it so badly before.'

Mike looked at her for a long moment. Was he wondering if her offer was genuine? Or wondering if she'd found something wrong with the land and was anxious to offload it in a hurry?

'Naturally, your father will have the chance to inspect the land before he buys,' she said stiffly. 'Or you can check it for him. As you must know, it's a prime piece of land. Those river flats in that wide loop of the river are ideal for cattle.' She rose as she spoke. 'Coffee?' she asked, clearing away the plates and dumping them in the sink.

'Thanks, I will.' Then, after a pause, he asked, 'Are you sure this is what you really want, Taryn? To sell off Plane Tree Flats? And the house? How do your young couple feel about it? Don't *they* want to buy it themselves, to start up a farm of their own?'

'Dino and Abby have agreed to help me with my new venture.' She hadn't offered the land to Dino...not that he could have afforded to buy a farm of his own just yet. She'd wanted to return Plane Tree Flats to its rightful owners...the O'Malleys. She wouldn't be needing the land, now that she was selling off her father's cattle.

'They'll be living here at Fernlea, in the loft above the stables,' she told him. 'We've been using it for guests, so it's already restored to the way it used to be. In fact it's *more* comfortable than it used to be.'

'Your new venture...' Mike's eyes narrowed speculatively. 'What precisely *is* your new venture?'

She lifted her chin. 'I'm turning Fernlea into an equestrian centre...a training and agistment centre for thoroughbred show-jumpers.'

Seconds ticked by before he commented. 'Well...that sounds like a full-time job...for someone. You're hiring experts to run the place? At least when you're not here?'

She tossed him a withering glance. '*I'll* be the full-time expert in charge...with Dino as my chief groom and right-hand man. And Abby—who happens to be a fine horsewoman herself—will help me exercise and train the horses. We'll all help with the grooming, feeding and mucking out.'

Mike shifted in his chair. '*You'll* be the full-time expert? You're saying you'll be staying down here *full-time*? To *work*?'

She dragged in a deep breath. 'You've always seen me as a spoilt, idle pleasure-seeker, haven't you, Michael O'Malley? You think I've been indulged all my life by doting parents and never had to lift a finger. Well, for your information, I'm already living and working here full-time...' she stressed the word 'working' '...now that I'm fully recovered from the accident. And

I intend to get my new enterprise underway without delay.'

'I'm glad you've made a full recovery, Taryn.' He smiled...a real smile this time, of heart-stopping warmth. Glancing up at her from his chair, he asked, 'You hurt your leg in the accident?'

It was asked in such a natural, matter-of-fact way that she heard herself answering in the same offhand way. 'Not my leg, just my foot. It was crushed when I was trapped in the car. The nerves and muscles were too damaged to repair completely. I'll always have a limp, though it may get less noticeable in time, as it strengthens.' Her chin lifted. 'I can still ride. Still jump. Still do anything but compete professionally.'

His eyes sought hers. 'That's why you gave up your show-jumping career? Not because—' He stopped. *Not because you found it too difficult or too daunting?* Was that what he'd been about to say?

Before she had a chance to ask, he muttered with a shake of his head, 'I can't quite work you out. You seem so...so...' He shrugged, and spread his hands.

'So like Crystal?' The question popped out, the bitterness from fourteen months ago flashing in her eyes.

He was staring at her. Blankly. Plainly shocked. 'What the hell makes you say that?' His brows knitted. 'What do *you* know about Crystal?'

'Nothing.' She tried to maintain her cool—at least outwardly. She had no intention of telling him that she knew about Crystal's return home last summer. Or about Mike's sleazy fling with her. 'Only that your father mistook me for someone called Crystal last year...when I drove you home the night we met. And I wondered who she was.'

'Oh...that. Forget it. It was a dumb mistake. You both have dark eyes and black hair...that's about the only similarity.'

'Tell me about her,' Taryn said, her face as impassive as she could manage. Having a look-alike—someone she could be mistaken for—was an odd sort of feeling. An uncomfortable feeling, knowing Mike's past involvement with Crystal. Especially last *summer's* involvement.

His face hardened as he answered, his eyes hooded now. 'Crystal *was*...at one time...' he stressed the past tense '...my fiancée.'

She schooled her face to show no reaction. 'But you broke off the engagement?' she prompted coolly. Had Crystal two-timed him, and he'd found out? Judging by his father's irate reaction last summer, when he'd mistaken her for Crystal, his future bride must have done something pretty nasty. Their break-up had really hurt him, Rory Silverman had said.

'*She* broke it off,' Mike corrected her, his face stony.

Because she'd fallen for another man? Taryn wondered. The man she later married? She searched his face in vain for a clue. Was there any lingering pain or anger—*or lingering passion*—under that coldly inscrutable mask? Or was he finally over her?

Did he regret his moment of weakness last summer?

Her mind flashed back to the day they first met. To the cynical gibes he hadn't been able to resist. 'Did she by any chance happen to be rich, spoilt, and involved in some way with horses and show-jumping?' she hazarded, her eyes narrowing.

A ghost of a smile drifted across his lips. 'You're trying to account for the chip on my shoulder you once accused me of having?' He gave a shrug. 'Very astute of you, Taryn. As if happens, Crystal's parents *are* wealthy...yes, though they're divorced now. Her mother's married again and is living in Spain. Her father—who dotes on his only daughter—owns a beef and thoroughbred horse stud near Korumburra...'

Korumburra! Taryn's stomach coiled into a knot at the mention of the town where Mike had met up again with his old flame last summer…where his feelings for Crystal had flared out of control. Rory had said Mike was probably disgusted with himself now. *Was* he?

'Crystal was never a show-jumper, but she did do a bit of dressage, although she never achieved great heights.' He spoke tonelessly, giving no clue to his feelings. 'She had other things she enjoyed doing more.' It was hard to tell if the faint twist at the corner of his lip was disapproval…or regret. 'She's married now and living overseas.'

Taryn kept her face deadpan, showing no sign of the sudden lift in her spirits. Not only was his ex-fiancée still married and still living overseas, but Mike had just explained away his past hostility towards. *her*, Hugh Conway's daughter. Both she and Crystal—who'd jilted him, presumably, for the man she'd since married—had more than just looks in common. They were both from wealthy families, both had doting fathers who owned cattle, both were mad on horses, and both had competed in the show-ring. No wonder Mike had been wary and mistrustful when he'd found out who she was.

But—she felt herself trembling—even if they did manage to become friends, would she ever be able to trust him? If he could succumb to his ex-fiancée after she'd jilted him for another man…if he could be attracted and repelled at the same time by a woman who'd bitterly hurt him…

She sighed. Did he deserve a chance…or not?

'Satisfied?' Mike said dryly. 'Now…how about we talk about something else? Tell me about your plans, Taryn…in more detail. Just what's involved?'

She would much rather have talked about his current feelings for his ex-fiancée…or about *his* plans, whatever they were. She was itching to know how long he intended to stay at home this time...if she would see him again after tonight. Or would he be gone again in a day or so, now that he'd seen his father? Heading back to Holland...or somewhere else?

But the questions would have to wait for now. He was waiting to hear about her new venture...wondering, no doubt, how it might affect the O'Malleys.

By the time they'd finished their coffee, she'd told him everything she planned to do. How she planned to purchase and train thoroughbred horses and then sell them as show-jumpers...how she planned to agist other people's horses, and to train them as show-jumpers, if they wished...and how she planned, eventually, to teach students. Mike had listened keenly from start to finish, surprising her by giving encouraging nods and even making a few helpful comments.

So different, she mused, from her mother and her friends and relatives back in town, who thought she was mad to take on such a demanding workload when she could have sold up and taken things easy back in Melbourne...or settled down with one of her city admirers. Despite her injury, she was still considered a good catch.

No one, not even her mother, understood her...or her real needs. Her father was the only one who ever had...who'd ever encouraged her love of horses and the country lifestyle that meant so much to her. Her mother had enjoyed boasting about her successes in the arena, and showing off her rosettes and trophies, but she'd never been interested in the hard work or long hours that had led to her triumphs.

And she certainly didn't want to hear about the hard work and long hours involved in her daughter's latest madness.

Taryn blinked rapidly, to clear a faint mistiness in her eyes. She still missed her father so much.

'I must be off,' Mike said, rising from the table. 'You've had a long day and must be tired.'

Her head jerked up. Had he seen the fluttering of her eyelashes and put it down to fatigue? Or was he simply seizing the opportunity to leave...now that he'd found out what he'd come to find out? That was more like it.

'Well, I do have a few things to do,' she said lightly, not wanting to hold him up...or to admit to being tired. Which she wasn't. Well, no more than usual at this hour of the day. She moved towards the door and pulled it open. 'I hope your father's well enough to come home tomorrow, Mike.' She hesitated, then asked, 'Will you be home for a while to take care of him?'

'I'm back for good,' Mike said easily, and she gripped the doorknob, her gaze leaping to his. Was he intending to take over his father's dairy farm after all? Or did 'back' and 'home' simply mean back in Australia...not necessarily living at the O'Malleys' farm next door?

'To work as a chemical engineer, a vet, or a dairy farmer?' she asked in a flippant tone.

He paused at the doorway. 'I guess you could say a bit of each...though breeder might be more accurate. I'll be working from home. Dad will still run his own dairy herd, while I—' He broke off, his lip quirking. 'But you have things to do. I won't bore you with the details now,' he said, to her frustration. 'I've held you up quite long enough. Thanks for the omelette, Taryn...it was delicious. See you around.'

'See you,' she said carelessly, reaching up automatically to switch on the lights in the yard as he stepped past her, out into the velvety night. She stood at the open doorway, ready to close the door after him. But instead of striding off he swung round to face her.

'I owe you an apology, don't I?'

Her heart thudded. 'What for?'

A wry smile tugged at his lips. 'For thinking you were

nothing but a pampered socialite who'd had everything handed to you on a silver platter. A spoilt rich kid who'd never had to work hard for anything.'

Like Crystal?

'Oh?' She lifted her chin, her eyes glinting as they met his. Underneath she didn't feel so cool. Her insides felt suddenly chaotic. So his opinion of her had changed, had it? 'You think there might be more to me?' she asked, widening her eyes. *Let him grovel,* she thought. It was what she'd always wanted to see.

'Oh, I'm sure there is…possibly far more than you've already revealed. You've quite won over my father…and not just because of your offer of the land. He was touched that you came in to visit him in hospital. And he likes your sense of humour. He enjoyed your joke about the heart surgeon…and was chuffed by the choice of reading matter you brought into hospital to cheer him up.'

His hands slid over her shoulders, his long fingers curling round them, warm and strong and oddly arousing. 'I underestimated you…implying that you'd never had to lift a finger or fight for anything in your life. You're tougher than I thought. You've fought your way back from serious injury. You're running your own property. And this new equestrian centre of yours would daunt even the hardest worker…the toughest, keenest horse*man*.'

His thumbs were massaging her shoulders, making it hard for her to think. 'Forgive me?' His face was so close she could feel his breath mingling with hers…warm, spicy, mildly tangy from the wine. 'Would a kiss help?' His eyes glittered above hers. 'You have the most irresistible lips.'

She gave a husky, nervous laugh. 'No need to go that far.' But she didn't turn away. She couldn't. Her eyes were mesmerised by the outline of his mouth, a breath away from hers. She knew she shouldn't listen to him, shouldn't let his sweet talk about irresistible lips seduce her, knowing how other lips had tempted him just as easily once. But she still didn't step away.

'What if I want to?' he murmured. Without waiting for an answer, he cupped her chin in his hand, bent his head and kissed her on the lips.

Instead of drawing back after the first light touch, his lips lingered, letting her taste their warm, sensual firmness. She felt her head spinning. This was no brief peck of apology...no token gesture of atonement. His mouth began to move over hers...gently...erotically. Tingles ran down her skin. Her breath quickened.

Feeling no resistance, his arms crushed her even closer, so close that she could feel the erratic beat of his heart. Or perhaps it was her own; it was hard to tell. His kisses became deeper, more insistent, his breath rasping against hers. She felt her own lips responding...not just her lips, but her body as well. Her chest rose and fell, her legs weakened beneath her, her veins flooded with heat. She heard a ringing in her ears...

A ringing that grew louder and more insistent.

She drew back sharply. 'My phone!'

'Great timing,' Mike growled, raising his head. His voice was thick, his breathing heavy. 'Maybe just as well.'

What did he mean by that? she wondered as she broke away from him with a gasped, 'Goodnight!' and whirled back inside to snatch up the kitchen phone. Was Mike *relieved* that their kiss had been interrupted...realising he'd let it get a bit out of hand? He probably hadn't expected such an eager response from her. *She* hadn't expected it either...responding to a man she wasn't sure she could even trust!

'Hullo?' She expected to hear her mother's voice. Or maybe Dino's. But it was someone totally unexpected.

'It's Smudge here…from the O'Malleys'. I'm looking for Mike. He said he was goin' to Fernlea. Is he still there?' The young man sounded breathless, agitated, his words tumbling over one another.

'Just a second… *Mike!*' she yelled, dropping the phone and rushing to the open door. 'Mike…*wait!*' He was halfway across the yard, but spun round as she called out. 'It's for you…it's Smudge. He sounds in a bit of a panic.'

In a few long strides, a tight-lipped Mike was back in her kitchen. She stood by as he rasped into the phone, 'What's happened? Are you… *What?* The *hospital*? Hell! What did they say? How bad is it?'

Oh, no, Taryn thought, clasping her chest. Not his father…not another heart attack!

She waited, holding her breath.

Mike crashed the receiver down. 'Dad's slipped in the bathroom and broken his hip. They're trying to find an orthopaedic surgeon. They hope he'll be able to operate first thing in the morning. I'd better get to the hospital and find out how bad it is.'

'Mike, I'm sorry. Is there anything I—'

'Nothing…thanks. I'll be in touch. See you!'

After he'd gone, Taryn's dazed thoughts dwelt for a while on poor Patrick, breaking his hip just as he was recovering from his heart attack. It wasn't fair. But then other, more turbulent thoughts pushed Mike's father to the back of her mind.

She found herself reliving that passionate kiss at her kitchen door…

She touched a finger to her lips. It wasn't the first time Mike O'Malley had kissed her. His kisses, she was finding, were like a drug…addictive. Powerfully addictive. After each one she wanted more…far more… whether they were good for her or not.

What would have happened if the phone hadn't rung?

Nothing, she suspected with a quivering sigh. He'd seemed relieved at the interruption. 'Maybe just as well,' he'd said. He'd only kissed her to show he no longer thought her a spoilt, pleasure-loving rich brat. He hadn't meant it to go as far as it had.

Unless it was pity that had prompted it...now that he knew her limp was permanent.

She'd encountered a lot of pity in the months since her accident...as well as other more galling reactions. Rory Silverman hadn't been the only man who'd been embarrassed to be seen with her. The males who'd pretended not to be, she cynically suspected, had most likely weighed her physical flaw against the Conway wealth and had only then decided to overlook it. She'd inherited more than just Fernlea and Plane Tree Flats from her father...he'd left her a wad of blue-chip shares as well. One day she'd inherit even more...unless her mother got so fed up with her she decided to disinherit her.

She smiled a twisted little smile. It had probably come close when she'd told her mother she was moving back to Fernlea...for good. Unsure of the people around her and missing her horses and the open country air, she hadn't been able to leave the city quickly enough. People in the country had different values, a different outlook on life. They were more honest and down-to-earth. More genuine. And her horses loved her just the way she was...unconditionally, flaws and all.

She blew out a sigh. Perhaps Mike was already regretting that impassioned kiss. Perhaps her reminder of Crystal, the woman he'd once loved and had held a torch for even after she'd ditched him for another man—a woman who apparently looked like *her*—had made him imagine for a few crazy seconds that *she* was Crystal...until the ringing phone had shattered the illusion and brought him back to earth.

Suddenly she felt very tired. Her foot was starting to ache, as it sometimes did after she'd been putting her weight on it for long periods at a time. She decided to have a long hot soaking bath and then crash into bed.

CHAPTER SEVEN

WHEN she came back to the house for breakfast in the morning, after doing her early morning chores, she dialled the O'Malleys' number, expecting to hear Mike's voice on the answering machine. He was bound to be at the hospital, or out in the yards with Smudge, but it was worth a try.

'Mike O'Malley.'

Her heart skipped a beat. 'Taryn.' She kept her tone cool, brisk. 'Any news on your father?' He'd said he would be in touch, but she'd found no message on her own machine.

'I was about to ring you... I've only just come back. They're operating on him now. He was in a lot of pain last night, but when I saw him again this morning he'd been sedated and was feeling drowsily out of it. He won't need a new hip, just a reduction, with some screws and plates. But he'll be out of action for quite a while.'

'Poor thing,' Taryn said, feeling for his father. She knew what being out of action was like. And crutches. And physio. And exercises. All of which Patrick would need in the weeks ahead. 'It must be a relief to him that you're back home, Mike. I won't go to see him until he's feeling up to having visitors, but I'll send some flowers to cheer him when he wakes up.'

She let her teeth tug at her lip, then asked, 'Will this put your own plans on hold? Your plans to go into...breeding?'

'No...not really.' He paused. 'I might call around to-night and tell you about it. But only if I can bring dinner.

I won't stay long… I've a meeting in Leongatha at eight.'

'There's no need to bring a meal with you.' Her pulses jumped at the thought of seeing him again, so soon. 'You'll have enough to do with your father and the—'

'I'll bring something from Warragul when I go to see Dad later this afternoon. No arguments. My father wants me to come and see you anyway. To discuss the sale. He's ready to buy as soon as you're ready to sell.'

'The sale? Oh…the land.' So that was the only reason he wanted to come and see her tonight. To discuss the sale. To get a firm commitment before she changed her mind and put Plane Tree Flats up for general sale…or put up the price. 'Right… I'll make sure I have all the information you want.' She spoke briskly, the way she spoke to business associates. 'Once we've agreed on the details, I'll get my solicitor to draw up a contract.'

'That sounds fine,' he said, and asked, 'Have you sold off all your cattle yet?' He was obviously just making conversation now, as beef cattle were of no interest to the O'Malleys. Unless…

'You're going into beef cattle?' she asked quickly. 'You're starting a beef stud?'

He laughed. 'Not quite. I was just wondering if you still had cattle on Plane Tree Flats, that's all…and how soon we'd be able to take possession. I realise Dino and Abby will have to move out of the house first.'

He sounded keen to get hold of the land that had once belonged to the O'Malleys. Did he need it for his new breeding venture? Or simply want to regain what he felt was rightfully theirs?

'I've sold off all but my father's prize Angus bull,' she told him. 'And someone's calling in later today to take a look at Senator with a view to buying.' Her stock station agent had called to warn her that the prospective buyer would be coming late this afternoon.

'You don't have to wait until we settle, Mike, before
you start using the land,' she heard herself offering im-
pulsively. 'You can put your cows down on Plane Tree
Flats now, if you like. Abby and Dino will be out of the
house by tomorrow—they've started moving their things
already—so you might as well make use of the land.'

'Thanks, Taryn... I might do that. It's good grazing
down there. We'll need to put a gate along the fence
somewhere... I could get Smudge to start work on that.'
He sounded pleased...as well he might, she thought. Not
only was Plane Tree Flats one of the richest pieces of
land around these parts, but he'd be getting it at a bar-
gain price.

Not that she regretted it for a second. She'd always
felt guilty about her father buying that piece of land over
Patrick O'Malley's head. Hugh Conway had paid a ridiculous price for it...which was a kind of justice in
itself.

'Well, good luck with the bull,' Mike said. 'See you,
Taryn... Don't work too hard.'

Don't *work* too hard? Hearing no mockery in his voice
encouraged her to enquire archly, 'You're actually ad-
vising the pampered Conway girl to ease back on her
workload?'

He gave a low chuckle. 'You still hold that against
me? Didn't I abase myself sufficiently last night?'

She went still. *Abase* himself? So that was all he'd
meant by that kiss! Nothing to do with irresistible
lips...or even with haunting images of his ex-fiancée.
He'd just felt he had to do some bowing and scraping!

'Grovelling doesn't suit you, Mike O'Malley.' She
spoke tartly. 'Luckily for you...' she assumed a cool
indifference '...I don't hold grudges.' *Not about that, at
any rate.*

'You're too kind. Look, I'd better get off the phone
in case the hospital rings.'

In case something goes wrong, he meant. 'He'll be fine, Mike,' she heard herself assuring him. 'He's pretty tough, your father.'

'I know. See you.'

'See you, Mike.' She hung up with a sigh.

She pointed Ginger in the direction of Plane Tree Flats, having decided to ride to the old house rather than drive there in the Land Cruiser. She hadn't been spending enough time lately with her favourite old show-jumper.

When they reached the dry grassy plateau on the way to the flats, she gave Ginger his head, keeping to the track she'd followed countless times before. She whooped aloud as he broke into a gallop, throwing back her head, loving the feel of the warm breeze in her face and through her hair, beneath her hard hat. It was another hot February day and any breeze was welcome.

Her spirits soared high as they thundered across the plateau, her face glowing, her eyes glistening with ex-hilaration, until a faint shadow flitted across her brow.

She just hoped Abby would be OK. It was bad luck, cutting her arm like that...on a nail that should never have been protruding in the first place. She'd never seen so much blood. Poor Abby was bound to need stitches. And probably a tetanus booster as well.

Dino had rushed Abby to their local doctor to have it seen to, which was why *she* was on her way to the old house. To keep an appointment for Abby.

By now they were flying down the slope towards the river, heading for the concrete bridge her father had put in between Fernlea and Plane Tree Flats. She glimpsed a young wombat, sitting like a big brown ball under a tree. After reading the *Muddle-headed Wombat* books as a child, she'd always had a soft spot for wombats—until she'd come to Fernlea and seen the damage they could cause, their huge holes causing soil erosion and posing hazards for her horses. But it was safe here on the track.

Directly ahead she could see the two enormous old plane trees after which the flats had been named, standing like giant sentinels on either side of the bridge. This summer, with the river down to a trickle, she could have crossed it almost anywhere.

She steered Ginger across the bridge to the lush flats beyond. Not so lush this summer, due to the hot winds and lack of rain, but still greener than the parched hills behind. She pointed the gelding in the direction of the old house up on the hill. The house that would soon belong to the O'Malleys.

To her right, a post-and-wire fence ran across the flats then up the hill, dividing Plane Tree Flats from the O'Malleys' property next door. Her heart jumped when she spied Mike's old ute near a new gap in the fence, and a man in a wide-brimmed hat crouched down near one of the fence posts. But when he glanced up she saw that it was Smudge.

As her spirits dipped slightly—foolishly—she caught a movement out of the corner of her eye. Someone on a big black horse was approaching Smudge from behind...from the direction of the O'Malleys'.

It was Mike on Caesar!

She took a deep breath and veered right, waving a hand to catch his attention. They met at the fence.

'You did say we could build a gate,' Mike reminded her, his eyes slightly guarded, she thought, under the brim of his shady Akubra hat. Was he expecting her to change her mind and order him off her land until the papers were signed?

'Of course you can. Did you think I'd come to stop you?' she said rather fractiously. Would he always think the worst of her? 'I just wanted to ask you how Patrick's operation went. Have you heard yet?'

He nodded, his mouth easing into a smile. 'It went without a hitch, thank God. They said I could come and see him in an hour or so. Not that he'll know much, but it'll reassure *me*...I hope.'

'That's great.' She squinted across the short distance between them. Nobody could doubt Mike's love for his father. Those rumours in the past about him deserting his father to follow his own selfish interests just didn't seem to jell any more. And Patrick had spoken so fondly of his son, so proudly, when she'd popped in to see him. It was obvious *he'd* never felt slighted.

'You're just out for a ride?' Mike asked pleasantly.

Her mellow musings evaporated. Did he think she had nothing better to do? Or that she'd just ridden to Plane Tree Flats to keep an eye on what *he* was doing?

'I've an appointment with someone, actually, at eleven,' she said coolly. 'Or rather I'm keeping an appointment for Abby. She's cut her arm and Dino's taken her to the doctor.'

'That's unfortunate. You're meeting someone at the old house?' he asked.

She nodded. 'An antique dealer. Abby and Dino want to sell off a couple of old pieces of furniture—good pieces that they inherited and don't really like—and someone's coming to value them. The loft is already furnished, you see, and they want to get rid of some of their old furniture.'

'Mm.' He was looking beyond her now. 'I think he's just arriving.' She saw his eyes narrow as she watched, saw his expression change, his jaw harden. 'Don't tell me Rory Silverman is in the antique business these days?'

Her head whipped round. A car was just turning into the drive of the old house further up the hill. Her eyes flared. There was no mistaking that bright red Porsche.

There couldn't be *two* in the area. That would be too much of a coincidence!

'I... Not as far as I know,' she faltered. She could feel Mike's eyes on her face. Was he wondering if he could believe her?

'No? Then it must be just a neighbourly call.' Mike's eyes chilled as her gaze swung back to his. 'Someone must have told him you were on your way to Plane Tree Flats.'

Her eyes flickered under his. Had Abby or Dino told Rory where she'd be, before they went off to the doctor's?

'You'd better not keep him waiting.'

She shivered under the coldness in his voice, in his eyes. He sounded more weary—disillusioned—than mocking. She was amazed at the sharp pang she felt. 'No... I guess not.' She glanced up the hill. The car was out of sight now behind the house, parked somewhere in the shade, no doubt.

As she prodded Ginger with her knees she saw that Mike had already turned away. Damn Rory Silverman, she cursed under her breath as she urged the gelding up the hill.

Would Mike still come to Fernlea tonight? She sighed. If he did, it would only be to finalise the sale of the land, not to be chummy and bring dinner. He would conveniently forget about that!

Damn!

She was ready to spit fire at Rory Silverman when she came face to face with him, but the man lolling against the red Porsche wasn't Rory!

'Anthony Cummings,' he introduced himself. A dapper young man in an expensive grey suit. 'You must be Abby...'

'Taryn Conway,' she said, blinking faintly. As she briefly explained what had happened to Abby, her eyes kept straying to the red Porsche, until Mr Cummings explained, almost apologetically. 'It's second-hand, not the latest model. I bought it from Rory Silverman, the polo player. He's bought himself a new one.'

Her breath hissed out. She even smiled. Such a simple explanation! And there was Mike down the hill, thinking she was having a cosy assignation up here with Rory Silverman!

It was tempting to let him go on believing it, but by the time she set off down the hill twenty minutes later she'd realised she didn't *want* Mike to go on thinking she was encouraging Rory Silverman's advances. Her eyes scanned the fence, hoping he'd still be there.

He was, but he'd remounted Caesar and was about to head off home, leaving Smudge still working on the new gate.

Mike paused as she brought Ginger to a halt near the gap in the fence. She realised her heart had picked up a beat. Would the truth make any difference to him? Would he even care?

'That was quick.' His tone was coolly sardonic, making her wish she'd stayed at the house for another twenty minutes, just to make him sweat. The thought of Mike O'Malley sweating over what she might or might not have been doing with Rory Silverman made her want to laugh. Hollowly.

'What happened to the antique dealer?' Mike asked, and she noted that the old bantering note was back. 'Don't tell me Rory *was* the antique dealer?'

Was he hoping that she'd say yes, that Rory had just come on business…to see Abby, not her? She let him wait a moment or two before she said coolly, 'No, Rory Silverman hasn't taken up dealing in antiques…' She paused. 'But he *has* sold his Porsche to an antique dealer by the name of Anthony Cummings.'

Her eyes danced a little as she let that sink in.

'Um…are you still coming around tonight, Mike?' she asked sweetly. 'To finalise the sale?' she was quick to add.

'I promised to bring dinner, remember?' he drawled. A promise is a promise, his eyes were saying. She couldn't read what else they might be saying, but the coldness and banter appeared to have gone. For now, at any rate.

She realised she was breathing more freely. 'Well, I'd better go,' she said. 'I want to ring the vet.'

'The vet? What's the problem?'

Her eyes leapt back to his. Of course… Mike was a vet himself, she remembered. She chewed on her lip. 'It may be nothing at all… I just want to be sure, that's all. Someone's coming to look at our bull later this afternoon,' she explained, 'and I thought he was looking a bit listless this morning. I already have the vet's certificate saying he's fine, but—'

'I'll ride back with you,' Mike sliced in, 'and check him over for you.'

Her eyes widened. He'd do that for her? 'Oh, no, I can't ask you to do that,' she protested, knowing he must be anxious to get to the hospital. 'You have enough to do…'

'You didn't ask… I offered. Come on, let's go. I'll race you.' His eyes challenged her.

'Oh, you will, will you? Come on, Ginger! *Go!*'

The two horses galloped off down the hill, Ginger crossing the bridge first. Taryn let out a gleeful laugh as the gelding flew up the track towards Fernlea, with Caesar at his heels.

When they reached the plateau, she glanced behind to see Caesar suddenly veer off the track, taking a short cut across the grassy expanse, weaving through the trees.

'You *rat!*' she shouted, and swung Ginger round to

follow him, screeching a warning as she closed the gap between them. 'Watch out for wombat holes!'

Her cry came a second too late. She saw Caesar swerve sharply, obviously to avoid one of the huge holes that were one of the main dangers on the property. The big black horse stumbled as he swerved, pitching Mike over his head.

'Mike!' She screamed in horror as Mike landed head-first in the grass, his Akubra hat hopefully softening the impact. Caesar had righted himself almost immediately, and now stood patiently waiting for Mike to get up.

He didn't.

Taryn's chest tightened, her heart in her mouth. Was he just stunned? Or seriously hurt? Or... 'Oh, dear God, no!' she moaned, sliding from the saddle as she brought Ginger to a running halt. Not *dead*!

She dropped to her knees beside him. Somehow, as he'd fallen, he'd rolled over onto his back. His eyes were closed and he was deathly still. Ripping off her hard hat and tossing it aside, she lowered her face to his, listening to see if he was still breathing. Her heart stopped. She couldn't detect any breath at all!

Her heart started again with a jolt, beating wildly, frantically. She mightn't have much time! Tilting his head back, she gently prised open his mouth and brought her own mouth down on his.

In the same moment his breath rasped from his lungs, his mouth came to life under hers, and a strongly mus-cled arm curled round her neck.

For a weak, insane second all she could think about was the feel of his lips on hers...warmly alive... blazingly sensual...piercingly erotic...making her want to taste them again...and again.

But only for a second.

She wrenched her mouth away. 'You *wretch*! You *tricked* me! You low-down, miserable, conniving—'

His lips stopped her, his hand clutching the back of her head, tangling in her hair, his other arm like a vice across her back. Again she felt her senses reeling, the sensual warmth of his lips paralysing her, their moist heat sending exquisite sensations coiling all the way through her.

Somehow, still kissing her, he rolled her over, so that now she was the one lying on her back, and he the one on top. His eyes laughed into hers as he finally drew back his head.

'Do you have a sense of *déjà vu*?' he murmured. 'Only this time it was *you* kissing *me* awake...' His mouth curved. 'Now I know how the sleeping beauty must have felt.'

'*Oh!*' Incensed, she pushed against his chest with all her strength, somehow managing to wriggle free. As she scrambled to her feet, snatching up her hard hat, she hissed, 'I was giving you mouth-to-mouth, you ungrateful good-for-nothing, not kissing you!'

'Really? You forgot to pinch my nose.'

'*Oh!*' she exploded again. 'You impossible—'

'*Please!*' he begged, holding up a hand. 'I can't take any more of these insults!'

She clamped the hard hat down on her head and grabbed Ginger's reins. 'I wouldn't waste any more of my breath!' Her face felt hot as she hauled herself up into the saddle. She was thinking of the breath she'd wasted on that kiss. 'Are you coming to see my bull or not?'

'Anything you say, ma'am.' He brushed himself down, righted his Akubra hat and headed for the happily grazing Caesar.

Taryn was already galloping off.

There was one more indignity waiting for her— though it came as a relief at the same time. When Mike examined her father's big black Angus bull in the yard where they'd brought Senator earlier in the day, he found nothing wrong with him...nothing at all.

'No, he's fine. In perfect nick.' Mike climbed the fence and jumped down to join her. 'Maybe he just seemed a bit listless because of the heat.'

Or maybe she'd imagined it, he might just as well have said. She felt her cheeks burning again. The arrival of Abby and Dino in Dino's old ute was a welcome diversion.

'I'd better find out how Abby is,' she said quickly. 'And give her the good news about her furniture.'

'And I'd better be off to the hospital,' said Mike, re-mounting Caesar. 'See you this evening, Taryn. I'm bringing dinner, remember.'

So he hadn't forgotten his promise. No, he'd want to keep her sweet until the papers were safely signed! She flushed, wondering if she was being unfair to him. But he made her so hopping mad sometimes! He made her feel... She tossed her head as she raised her hand in a brief salute. He made her feel...

She sighed.

He made her feel a whole gamut of conflicting emotions!

CHAPTER EIGHT

THE prospective buyer didn't arrive to look at the bull until the sun was low in the hazy blue sky and the shadows in the yard were lengthening.

'Miss Conway...delighted to meet you.' He was a big, powerfully built man of about sixty with thick silver-grey hair, dark brown eyes and a strong face that must have been devastatingly handsome in his younger years. All she knew about him was that he owned a cattle property in South Gippsland somewhere and that his name was Curtis Bannister.

'Please...call me Taryn,' she said as she shook his hand.

He gave her a quick, intent look—was he surprised to find a young woman in charge of a property, or was he thinking that first names were too familiar?—before muttering, 'Fine, fine,' without inviting her to call him Curtis in return.

He had a young woman with him, who was alighting from the passenger's side of his silver-green Mercedes. She looked eye-catchingly attractive in a daffodil-yellow shirt and pale clinging jodhpurs. Taryn was just wondering if it was his wife—a much younger second wife, perhaps—when the big man turned and with a beaming smile, introduced her.

'My daughter... Crystal.'

Crystal? Taryn's mouth went dry. It couldn't be *that* Crystal. Mike's ex-fiancée was married and living overseas. But she knew, the moment the girl removed her dark glasses and they came face to face, that it *was*.

It wasn't quite like looking in a mirror, but the likeness was striking. Both of them had wide-set black eyes under dark winged brows, both had full, gently curved lips—Crystal's enhanced with bright red lipstick—and both were tall and slender with glossy shoulder-length black hair—though her own, today, was pulled back in a ponytail. The girl even had a dimple, just as she had, in her small pointed chin.

For a second or two they stood staring at each other. Clearly, Crystal had noted the similarity too—as her father, with that intent look a moment ago, must have too. The girl didn't say anything, but her dark eyelashes flickered and her mouth tightened imperceptibly, as if she was unamused at the similarity. Unless she simply disliked being in the company of an equally attractive woman.

'Nice to meet you...Crystal,' Taryn forced out, only now noticing that the girl wore no wedding ring. She swallowed. Had the girl's marriage already broken down? Her heart sank a little.

Approaching footsteps gave her a chance to turn away. 'Ah, Dino...' She beckoned him forward. 'I'd like you to meet Curtis Bannister...and his daughter Crystal. Dino will take you to the cattle yard, Mr Bannister, where Senator is. And he has the vet's certificate to show you. If you're interested in buying the bull, Dino will bring you back here, and we'll talk business.'

'Perhaps, while my father is looking at the bull,' Crystal put in with an enchanting smile that Taryn imagined would be hard for anyone, especially a man, to resist, 'you wouldn't mind showing me your horses, Miss Conway?'

Taryn hesitated, but only for a second. Crystal's family, Mike had told her, owned a beef and thoroughbred horse stud near Korumburra, not too far from here. It was possible that she might want to buy a horse from them one day...or the Bannisters might give her equestrian centre some valuable publicity, by mentioning it to their friends and clients. She'd be mad to alienate them.

'Well…they're out in the paddock at the moment,' she told the girl, 'but we can wander over and take a look…certainly. And it's Taryn,' she added, keeping her tone light. 'You don't mind if I call you Crystal?' Curtis Bannister hadn't actually mentioned his daughter's surname. Presumably she'd changed it when she married. Or had she kept her maiden name? Or reverted to it since?

The girl shrugged. 'Be my guest.' The smile had gone, from her lips as well as her eyes, now that Taryn had given in to her request.

Taryn led the way…conscious, as she glanced round at one stage, that Crystal's gaze was fixed to her right foot. Her *lame* foot. She caught a very different smile on the girl's lips this time…a derisive little smile…and didn't miss the disdainful gleam in the dark gaze as it flicked away.

So now she no longer sees me as competition, Taryn thought with a tight little smile of her own. *I'm flawed.* She felt her heart twist a little. Did Mike see her as flawed too? A lot of men did.

She didn't attempt to make conversation until they reached the home paddock. So far she wasn't terribly impressed with Mike O'Malley's ex-fiancée. What had attracted him to Crystal in the first place? Apart from a pretty face and a great figure. And a dazzling smile that the girl seemed able to turn on and off like a tap.

Perhaps she'd only ever shown Mike her charming, sparkly side. Perhaps he'd been so blinded by her beauty—by the surface dazzle—that he'd only realised after she'd jilted him for another man that she was really a spoilt, two-timing rich bitch, which had led to that chip on his shoulder and his cynicism about women he perceived to be like her.

Yet it didn't seem to have dampened his passion for his old flame, if last summer was anything to go by. Taryn's mouth hardened. Unless it had been a moment of madness he'd quickly regretted.

She heaved a sigh. Now that she'd seen Crystal for herself, and seen how alike they both were—on the surface, at least—she wondered if Mike would ever be able to see beyond Crystal's face when he looked at *her*. Whether he hated or still carried a torch for the girl made no difference. If he was reminded of his faithless ex-fiancée every time he looked at her... She shivered.

By now the sun was nudging the top of the hills, streaking the sky with wisps of pink and gold. It would be dark soon. She wondered what time Mike would arrive. He was bringing dinner, he'd said. She willed him not to come before the Bannisters had gone.

While they were leaning on the fence, fussing over her favourite old show-jumper, Ginger—who'd trotted straight up to the rail on sighting Taryn—Crystal said casually, 'I understand the O'Malleys are close neighbours of yours?'

Taryn's heart did a double flip in her chest. 'That's right,' she answered carefully. 'The O'Malleys own the dairy farm next door...across the river.' Was Crystal going to ask about Mike? Was that why she'd come here today with her father? To find out what her former fiancé was doing with himself these days? To find out if he was still free...or if he'd married someone else?

To find out if he was still in love with her?

A lump lodged in her throat. Perhaps, if Crystal's own marriage really *had* broken down, she'd come back hoping for a reconciliation. Would Mike take his ex-fiancée back if she *was* free, and making herself available? *Did* he still love her, deep down? If he hadn't been able to resist her when she was married, despite the hurt she'd caused him in the past, how would he be able to with-stand a *free* Crystal?

'But it's only Patrick O'Malley who lives there now, isn't it?' Crystal probed. 'His son's still away...isn't he? Mike and I used to be engaged, you know...a couple of years ago. After I broke it off—how I regret it now!—he went away...to work in the backblocks of Australia somewhere. The poor dear was heartbroken, everyone said.'

A sigh quivered from the bright lips. 'We were so right for each other...if I'd only realised it. But I was younger and more impetuous then and didn't know *what* I wanted. Later, after I married, we met up again...just once, early last summer, before he went off to America.' *So it was true!* 'The spark was still there,' she said dreamily, a faint glitter—of self-satisfaction?—in her dark eyes. 'Is he still away, do you know?'

So right for each other... The spark was still there... The poor dear was heartbroken... Taryn's mind spun. *Was* Mike heartbroken? she wondered, swallowing. Well, of course he must have been...being jilted like that. Jilted for another man. And now Crystal was having regrets about dumping him, was she? Did she also have ideas about winning him back?

'Actually, he's back home,' she answered, striving to speak normally. 'His father had a heart attack recently. Luckily it wasn't serious. Only now Patrick's broken his hip—in the hospital of all places—and is being—'

'Mike's *home*?' Crystal cut in, not interested in Patrick or his ailments. 'You've seen him?'

The way she asked that last question, with her black eyes boring into Taryn's, she might as well have asked, Has he seen *you*? There were vibes coming thick and fast from the girl...even though her face was a coolly controlled mask.

Taryn turned back to Ginger to avoid the girl's searing

scrutiny, trying to blot out the memory of Mike's lips on hers. 'A couple of times. He's only been back a few days,' she said evasively, and clenched her teeth, annoyed at herself for sounding so defensive. She wondered how Crystal would take it if she knew they'd met before...fourteen months ago. Mike was hardly likely to have told her.

'So... Mike's back home and his father's in hospital...' There was an undercurrent of elation in the girl's voice. Recalling Patrick's enraged reaction the night he'd mistakenly thought Crystal had come back into their lives, Taryn could understand why. The old man was out of the way. Mike was home alone.

She was relieved to see Curtis Bannister and Dino approaching, both looking well satisfied. Curtis had decided to buy the bull.

'He's a fine animal,' he said, beaming. 'Good structure. Good feet. Walks well...excellently, in fact.' He raised bushy eyebrows. 'You have the documents ready? If so, I'll give you a cheque straightaway—I don't intend to haggle—and I'll send transport to pick him up tomorrow.'

Taryn nodded, hiding a faint smile. She'd put a fixed price on the bull—a realistic price, not an exorbitant one—and had told her stock station agent to make it clear to prospective buyers that it was that or nothing. It was simpler that way.

'I have all his papers in my office,' she told Curtis. 'And my solicitor has prepared the contract of sale for you to sign. Shall we go inside?'

They went into the house to sign the deal. She took them in by the front door, which she seldom used herself...steering them through the spacious hall, with its leadlight windows, patterned floor rugs, pressed-metal ceiling and winding cedar staircase, before passing through a corbelled circular arch into the picture-lined passage leading to the office, a couple of doors along.

'Nice place,' Crystal remarked without a flicker of warmth. 'You're intending to sell up, Taryn, once you get rid of the bull...and your horses?'

'No, not at all,' Taryn answered evenly. 'I won't be selling Fernlea...*or* my horses. In fact, I'll be adding to them. I'm starting up a training and agistment centre...for thoroughbred show-jumpers.'

'Really?' Crystal looked pointedly at her foot. 'But you'll have someone else to run it, won't you? *You* won't be training horses...or even living here full-time...surely? Isn't your real home in the city?'

Taryn clenched her teeth. Did the girl have to keep reminding her, so blatantly, that she had an impediment? 'On the contrary, I'll be living here full-time and doing everything...with the help of Dino and his wife, Abby. I'm still capable of riding...even jumping. Once the new jumping courses and circular lunging track are finished, and the new fenced paddocks are ready for the additional horses, I'll be underway. I've already advertised in the equestrian journals and local newspapers.'

'Really?' Crystal said again, more thoughtfully this time. 'You honestly think you can make a go of it? Running an equestrian centre would be hard work even for an *un*handicapped person. But being disabled... I hope you realise what you're taking on, Taryn?'

Taryn kept her cool with sheer effort of will. It was the first time anyone had called her handicapped to her face...though she guessed it wouldn't be the last.

She forced a grim half-smile, not bothering to answer, thankful that Dino was talking to Curtis Bannister.

'You live here alone?' Crystal's eyes pinned hers. 'There's no...husband? Live-in boyfriend?' She dropped her voice and smiled as she said it, as if this were a chummy girl-to-girl chat.

Taryn took a deep breath, wondering why she would want to know that. But when she answered her eyes didn't waver. 'No...there's no husband.' Whether she had a live-in boyfriend or not was no business of Crystal's. Did the girl think she might already have taken up with her next-door neighbour?

She moved forward to give Curtis Bannister her attention. Once the papers were signed and the transport of the bull had been arranged, she saw them both out, while Dino strode off to where he'd left his motorbike. By now dusk was falling, and the light was beginning to fade.

As she escorted father and daughter across the yard to the Mercedes, she heard the sound of a throbbing engine and a grey Range Rover careered into the yard, swerving to avoid the Mercedes. It was Mike!

She stifled a groan. Why couldn't he have stayed away for another five minutes? Or even three minutes? Damn!

He pulled up...far closer than she would have wished. She willed him to stay in his car until her visitors had gone. But Crystal, it seemed, had other ideas. She'd come to an abrupt halt, and was peering at the man in the driver's seat. Even in the growing gloom, her face seemed to blanch.

'Mike? Is that Mike O'Malley?' Her head whipped round to face her, and in the instant their eyes met Taryn caught a gleam of something close to malice in the glittering dark gaze. 'It *is* Mike...isn't it?'

The girl's eyes seemed to be demanding, What's my ex-fiancé doing here...calling on *you* at this late hour of the day?

Taryn had a feeling she was also thinking, If he's stupid enough to be attracted to a lame duck like you, it can only be because you look a bit like me.

She schooled her expression to show none of the emotions that were swirling inside her. 'The O'Malleys are buying some land from me,' she said airily, omitting to mention that Mike had offered to bring dinner—if he'd remembered. She just hoped he wouldn't step out of the Range Rover with a pizza box in his arms!

He did step out...but he wasn't carrying any boxes. Taryn felt a wobbly sensation inside as his great shoulders emerged, and his long, jean-clad legs. His hair, wild as ever, gave him a rakish, untamed look as he strode straight over to them, his expression unreadable in the fading light.

'Well...Curtis...Crystal...fancy seeing you here.' Ignoring Crystal for the moment, he held out his hand to Curtis, who, after the faintest hesitation, gripped it in the briefest of shakes.

'We're here to buy Miss Conway's bull,' Curtis said gruffly. 'Didn't expect to see *you* here.' He glanced at his daughter, as if wondering, suddenly, if she'd known her ex-fiancé was back in Australia and if she'd come with him to Fernlea knowing the O'Malley dairy farm was next door.

'Mike!' Crystal gave a tinkling cry and pranced forward to grip his forearm with long, red-tipped fingers. 'I don't believe it! Is it you? You're actually back home?'

Taryn blinked at the transformation in the girl. She was all sweetness and light now, all bubbly charm, her lovely face glowing with a heart-jolting radiance, even in the dimness. If Mike had only ever seen this side of the girl, she thought with a sick swoop of her stomach, no wonder he'd fallen in love with her.

Would he fall for her all over again?

'I've heard how well you've been doing, Mike.' Crystal's voice bubbled on. 'How you made an absolute fortune from that clever little device you invented...what was it again?'

'An injectable drench,' Mike said dryly. 'So you find it more appealing now, do you? Now that it's made me rich?'

'Oh, Mike,' the girl gurgled, letting a well-manicured hand flutter in the air, 'you can't blame me for finding a parasite-killing device just a *tiny* bit boring. Chemical drenches are hardly dinner party material—as I used to chide you, remember? But it didn't mean I wasn't proud of you, Mike. I'm simply delighted that you've done so well. Who would have guessed it would be so success-ful? All over the world!'

'Who indeed?' Mike's tone was heavy with irony. 'Success came after a lot of hard work and after a lot of time spent promoting it.'

'Yes, of *course*.' Crystal's eyes clung to his, limpid with admiration. 'Mike, I had no idea you were back home.' She dropped her voice to a husky whisper. 'I was wary of calling your father...knowing that he never particularly took to me.' She gave a trill of laughter, as if it were unthinkable that anyone wouldn't fall at her feet.

'So you thought you'd grill my neighbours.' Mike extricated his arm. He appeared unmoved by her warm welcome, impervious to her charms. Unless, Taryn thought bitterly, it was a steely cover for the attraction he still felt for her...an attraction he was trying to fight, knowing how she'd hurt him in the past...knowing how he'd already let her tempt him once since she'd walked out on him.

Curtis Bannister was already moving away, pulling open the driver's door of the Mercedes, his eyes willing his daughter to come with him. But she wasn't ready yet.

'Mike...don't be cruel.' She pouted charmingly. 'I came to Fernlea to keep my father company...you know how we always liked to do things together. And now that I'm home again...' A glowing smile lit her face. 'Well, naturally, when I realised Fernlea was next door to your old home, Mike, I was keen to ask after you...to find out how you're going and what you're doing with yourself these days...'

'To find out if I'd found someone else to marry...like you did?' Mike's voice was cold, his eyes silvery glints in the failing light. 'How *is* your husband, by the way?'

'Mike, I left him. It was a terrible mistake... I should never have married him. I married on the rebound...you *know* that. I wanted to hit back at you, Mike, after our silly quarrel. We should never have split up, you and I.' She gazed up at him, her eyes like shining ebony, her glossy black hair cascading over the shoulders of her bright yellow shirt. 'There's no one to match you, Mike... I realised it too late.'

Taryn's heart missed a beat. The girl seemed oblivious of the fact that there was a third party present. Or perhaps she was only too well aware. Her father, by now, was already sitting in the Mercedes, patiently waiting. Not wanting to hear any more, Taryn began to back away, but Mike's voice halted her.

'No need to go, Taryn... I'm coming.'

But Crystal hadn't finished. With a choked, almost pleading catch in her voice, she cried out, 'You can't blame me for leaving my husband, Mike. He's been charged with *fraud*, for heaven's sake. Can you believe it?'

'So you left him when he was down.' Mike eyed her stonily. 'Poor blighter.'

Had Crystal left Mike when *he* was down? Taryn wondered. He wouldn't have been rich and successful then...he hadn't launched his injectable drench until after their break-up.

'I was going to leave him anyway,' Crystal asserted.

'I never loved him, Mike. I've only ever loved one man...'

'Your father's waiting for you, Crystal.' Mike's tone was rock-hard, his face coldly implacable. 'Good*night*.' He swung away, raising a hand to her father in a brief salute as he strode off...sweeping Taryn towards the Range Rover—deliberately, perhaps, touching a hand to her back.

To show his ex-fiancée that they'd already become good friends? Taryn wondered unsteadily. Or was it meant to reassure *her*?

Or—her lips tightened—was it a calculated attempt to make his ex-fiancée jealous?

'I've take-away Chinese and a bottle of wine in the car,' he told her in a quite different tone now, all the coldness and rasping harshness gone, as if nothing had happened. 'Over our meal I'll tell you about my father's operation, and then all about...' she thought he was going to say 'my ex-fiancée', but what he said had nothing to do with Crystal '...the new venture I'm about to embark on.'

'Oh...yes, fine,' she said, wincing at the huskiness in her voice, her face averted from his. Was he going to avoid talking about his old flame altogether? Was that a good sign—a sign that he no longer cared about her?

Or a sign that he was still bitterly hurt and angry at what Crystal had done to him, and was trying not to show it by harshly repudiating the girl?

CHAPTER NINE

'YOU saw your father?' she asked Mike over their sweet-and-sour scallops. Foil containers packed with Mongolian lamb, Chinese vegetables and fried rice were still in the oven keeping warm.

'I did, and he's coming along fine. He was still groggy when I saw him, and on a drip, but was in no pain.'

'Oh, that's good.' They were in the den this time, their plates perched on their laps, wineglasses at hand. The den, with its comfy armchairs and book-cluttered walls, was cosier than the kitchen—and this time for some reason she'd wanted to be cosy. Unless it was just that the light in here was softer...less revealing.

'Did he get the flowers I sent him?' she asked. She'd rung a Warragul florist earlier in the day to arrange the delivery.

'He did, and he asked me to thank you. They were the first thing he saw, he said, when he woke up in his own room. He was quite overcome.'

She smiled, then, catching the warmth in his eyes, took a quick sip of her wine. 'When do you think he could have visitors?' she asked.

'Well, I'd wait for a day or so, but after that I'm sure he'd love to have a pretty visitor to perk him up, if you have the time. I know how busy you are, getting your new set-up underway. I'm going to be pretty flat out too, for a while.'

She went still. Was he already trying to ease himself out of her life...now that Crystal was back, and single again? The genuine article would be more attractive, no doubt, than the flawed imitation.

It was the first time she'd allowed any self-pity to creep into her thinking. Damn Crystal, she thought. And damn Mike too, if he preferred a woman like that fickle two-faced witch.

Did he? He'd shown only coldness and biting scorn when he and his old flame had come face to face earlier. But if he'd really loved Crystal in the past—if he'd been genuinely hurt when she'd tossed him over for another man—a self-protective mask of icy indifference would be understandable.

She nibbled on her lip as she slipped out to the kitchen to fetch their main course. But now that his old sweetheart was free again, and throwing herself at him, would his defences begin to crumble? Would he bury his bitterness and hurt, acknowledge his true feelings for Crystal, and decide to give her another chance?

'Well, now...' Mike smiled as she came back with their filled plates, seemingly unaware of her turbulent thoughts. 'I also promised I'd tell you about my own new venture.'

Shrugging off her morbid musings, she handed him his plate and sank into the same armchair as before, looking at him expectantly. 'You've decided to work with your father,' she prompted. Patrick must be pleased as punch, she thought, to have his son back home...for good this time. Especially with his bad heart, and now a broken hip. 'You mentioned you're going into breeding.'

'That's right. Dad will go on producing milk from his dairy farm, with Smudge's help, and I'll be concentrating on building up an élite dairy stud...importing the very best genetics from overseas.'

'Ah.' An élite dairy stud, using imported genetics. So that was it. She raised curious eyes to his—at the same time trying to read what might lie behind the keen blue depths. Haunting images of Crystal? 'Will you be using your father's cows?'

He nodded. 'I'll be using his best cows to get me started, impregnating them with imported semen—the very best available.' He paused, as if he thought he might be boring her. Her eyes encouraged him to go on. 'We'll flush the cows to produce the finest embryos possible. We also have the ability to import the very best embryos from overseas, particularly from Holland.'

'So…you must have been interested in dairy genetics for some time?' She winced as she remembered how she'd condemned him last year for looking down his nose at dairy farming and turning his back on his father.

Mike's lip twitched, as if he'd read her thoughts. 'I became involved in genetics at vet college. And in disease control as well. After I qualified I was head-hunted by an international research-based chemical company for the work I'd done on producing a new injectable drench. I did a chemical engineering course while I was perfecting it. I've spent the past couple of years promoting it round Australia and throughout America. It's been a stunning success.'

And made him a lot of money, according to Crystal…who, Taryn had a feeling, would gauge a man's worth by the amount of money he made. The more money, the more successful and desirable he'd be in her eyes.

Had he done it for Crystal? The question scraped to the surface. Only his fiancée hadn't waited around for long enough to benefit from his success. *But now that she was free again…*

She swallowed. 'But your real love is genetics?' she hazarded. 'That's why you came back?'

He looked at her for a long moment, causing her heart to start a slow thudding. 'Yes…genetics is where my real interest lies.'

He'd changed her word 'love' to 'interest', she noted. Because his *love* lay in another direction? She gulped as an image of Crystal's dazzling smile caused her eyes to waver under his.

'And I wanted to help my father, of course.' Mike's eyes glinted as he said it. 'He's had trouble obtaining the best genetics—they weren't available here in Australia—so I decided to import them myself. I've already set up an artificial breeding company—O'Malley's World Élite Genetics—and I'll be using the contacts I made overseas to source the very best genetics from Holland, Canada and America, to sell back here...as well as making use of them myself, to launch my own élite dairy stud.'

No wonder his days were so full. She inhaled deeply, then released her breath. 'Why didn't you tell me all this before? Why didn't you tell me when I accused you of turning up your nose at dairy farming...and walking out on your father?'

Amused satisfaction shimmered in his eyes. 'You were determined to cast me in the role of heartless prodigal son. It seemed pointless to defend myself.' His eyes narrowed. 'Did you bother to defend yourself against any of *my* misconceptions...of *you*?'

She reached for her glass, a rueful smile tugging at her lips. 'You were so determined to think badly of me...of all the Conways...that I thought, Why bother? That's the real reason you didn't tell me the truth about what you were doing...isn't it?' she challenged, glancing up at him through her thick lashes. 'You didn't think enough of me to care if I knew the truth or not.' *You thought I was too much like Crystal...beautiful, desirable, but untrustworthy.*

He didn't answer at once—which seemed an answer in itself. As she drained her glass and rose with a sigh to gather up their plates, he said slowly, seeming to pick his words, 'Oh, I thought enough of you, Taryn...too much. Those kissable lips of yours were nearly my undoing...that very first day in the pine forest.'

She paused in mid-step, her fingers tightening on the plates in her hand. 'Because I reminded you of your ex-fiancée?' She asked the question amazingly steadily, though inwardly she was trembling, her heartbeat unsteady, even while her heart turned to ice. Only two days later he'd sought *other* lips...very similar lips. *The lips he'd never stopped wanting?* 'We do look a bit alike...I saw that for myself.'

'Taryn—'

'No need to say anything,' she said in a rush, silently kicking herself for forcing an admission. Other admissions might follow and she didn't want to hear them. 'I'll get you some rice pudding and ice cream.' She'd baked the rice pudding earlier in the day, with loving care. It had been a favourite of her father's.

'Thanks, but I must be off, I'm afraid.' Mike was already on his feet. 'This meeting in Leongatha...it's time I was making tracks.'

'Oh, yes...you'd better.' She was breathily polite now. Would he have been in quite so much of a rush if she hadn't reminded him of Crystal, and the similarities between them? If she hadn't probed into his feelings?

He picked up the two empty wineglasses and followed her out to the kitchen, placing them on the sink as she stuck the plates in the dishwasher.

'Thanks for bringing the meal, Mike...it was delicious,' she said without turning back to him, expecting him to make a hasty farewell and head for the door. But he didn't. He caught her arm instead and gently urged her round to face him.

'Any similarity between you and my ex-fiancée,' he said deliberately, 'was far from my mind when I kissed you that day. I swear it.'

She forced her chin up...forced her eyes to meet his. 'But once you knew who I was—that I was Hugh Conway's daughter—the similarities must have struck you then. That it wasn't just looks we had in common, but family wealth and lifestyles as well. Even the same posh accent.' The Toorak twang, he'd called it.

He didn't deny it. But he did give her a brief, frustrated shake. 'You want me to apologise all over again for labelling you an idle, spoilt rich kid?'

She shook her head. She didn't want apologies....she wanted assurances. Assurances that he no longer cared about Crystal. But she couldn't ask for them. What right did she have?

'You weren't so wrong.' She half-laughed. 'My parents did spoil me... I didn't have a proper job...and we *were* rich. Please, just forget it. You'd better go or you'll be late for your meeting.'

He grimaced. 'You're right. I'm afraid this is a bad week. Tomorrow I'm not going to have time to breathe.'

She wondered if he was apologising again...or backing away. He would want time to think about Crystal, no doubt.

'Neither am I,' she said quickly, not wanting him to feel she expected anything of him. She *didn't*. She'd be mad to expect anything of a man who couldn't make up his mind if he desired a woman or despised her! 'The farrier's coming,' she rushed on, 'and a new horse that someone wants to keep here for a spell...and I have to go out to look at a mare that's for sale...as well as all the usual chores, and supervising the new cross-country course that Dino's working on...'

He looked into her eyes for a long charged moment, and she held her breath, thinking he was about to ask if she was up to all this, with her bad foot—she knew Crystal would have had no compunction about saying it outright—but Mike just smiled, and dropped a light kiss on her brow.

'You can tell me all about it later,' he said. For a second his hands tightened on her arms, then he released her, and swung away. Next moment he'd gone.

As she shut the door after him, she wondered with a sudden bleakness if there would be a later, or if he'd only said that for something to say, the way a person would say, We must keep in touch, without meaning a word of it.

He hadn't kissed her this time. You could hardly call that brotherly peck on the cheek a kiss. If he'd *wanted* to kiss her, even though he was in a hurry, he could have done a lot better than that. He could have kissed her on the *lips*, for a start.

Was his mind on his meeting in Leongatha? On his sick father? Or—she heaved a deep sigh—did she remind him too much of the woman he'd once loved...and might still love, under the coldness and cynicism? Was he haunted by the fact that his old flame was back home again...available again...and openly offering herself to him...as a free woman this time? Was his battered love for her already stirring again, ready to flare back to life?

Would the seductive lure of his ex-fiancée be too great? It had been once before. Why not again?

She had so much to do the next day, especially with two new horses to settle in during the afternoon, that she had no time to dwell on the questions simmering away inside her. It was late afternoon before she knew it.

A welcome breeze had blown in, a relief from the burning heat of the day. She looked hopefully up at the sky, but although there were a few scudding clouds there was no sign of rain. They badly needed it. The hills were depressingly dry and brown after the long hot summer, so different from the rich green of last year's unusually wet summer.

After bringing in the horses, she joined Abby in the stables to help with the last-minute chores. Dino was still working on the new cross-country course in the far paddocks, but he'd be coming in shortly.

While she was working outside Ginger's stall, picking out the gelding's hooves to remove any stones that might have lodged there, she heard a car drive into the yard.

Her head jerked up, hope lighting her eyes. Mike? The hope died when she saw an unfamiliar red Jaguar. Her spirits plunged even more when she saw Crystal climbing out...a vision of feminine allure in a figure-hugging red cropped top, pale leg-hugging jodhpurs, and embossed leather boots.

'Ah, there you are,' the girl trilled, sashaying—there was no other word for it—towards her.

Taryn summoned a smile, but kept on working. Why had the girl come back? To check if Mike was here?

'I just had to come back and see you,' Crystal gushed, glancing round as she approached—as if to make sure Mike wasn't hiding somewhere. 'I felt a bit bad about yesterday.'

Taryn glanced up with widening eyes. *Bad* about yesterday? The girl's lovely face was bland, her dark eyes more coolly watchful, she thought, than contrite.

'A bit bad...about what?' she asked warily.

'I'm afraid I wasn't very friendly yesterday. I guess I was just a teensy bit jealous,' the girl admitted. 'Seeing you with Mike. And seeing how alike we are, you and I. Mike must have seen it too...it's probably what attracted him to you.'

Taryn felt a little sick. Crystal was only echoing her own fears...despite Mike's attempts to play down any likeness between them. 'There's nothing between Mike and me.' She forced the words out. Knowing they were untrue…at least from her point of view. Mike already meant far too much…

Which was crazy, in light of what had happened last summer. He'd virtually gone straight from her to Crystal. He could do it again. Openly this time, now that his old flame was free. Just because he'd kissed her a couple of times, and had admitted that he'd been wrong about her that didn't mean he'd developed any real feelings for her.

'Anyway, I want to make it up to you,' Crystal insisted, turning to her with the full force of her lustrous black eyes. 'I'm here to offer my services.'

'Your…services?' Taryn blinked.

'I'm offering you my *help*, Taryn. With your training centre. As of right now.' She flashed a bright smile and waggled a hand, her gaze flickering past her. 'Can I exercise a horse or something? Or lunge your new mare? That *is* a new mare, isn't it?' She was watching Abby leading the handsome chestnut across the yard.

Taryn eyed Crystal for a bemused moment. 'We do all the training and exercising earlier in the day,' she told the girl. Surely, if Crystal had worked with horses at her father's stud, she would know that they wouldn't be doing it at this late hour?

'If you really want to do something to help,' she added slowly, lowering her lashes to hide an impish glint in her eye, 'you could go out into the home paddock and pick up their droppings. It's about the only thing we haven't done.'

'I'm not offering my services as a *groom*, Taryn.' The smile vanished, the red lips tightening. 'You have your girl and that Dino person to do that kind of thing. I'm offering my services as an able-bodied equestrian *expert*…something I'm sure you could do with.'

Able-bodied… Taryn fought down the surge of bile

that rose in her throat. The girl never missed a chance to remind her that she was less than perfect.

As she fought for her normal coolness, it struck her that Crystal had chosen a very strange time of day to come offering to help with the horses. Was she hoping that if she came late enough Mike might drop by, as he'd done around this time the previous day…and that he'd be impressed to find his old flame here lending a hand?

She could almost hear Crystal trilling to Mike, *Lending a hand is the least I can do to help poor brave Taryn get her ambitious project underway.* Implying that the poor creature needed all the *able-bodied* help she could get.

'Thanks, but I don't need any extra help at present,' Taryn said levelly.

'Taryn, I'm not expecting *payment*.' Crystal looked pained, almost tempting Taryn to retort, Oh, it's out of the goodness of your heart, is it?

Crystal didn't strike her as the type of person to do *anything* out of the goodness of her heart. She'd have a jolly good reason, and it would have nothing to do with wanting to make amends for yesterday…or wanting to help *her*.

As Crystal ambled past her to stroke Ginger's glossy neck, with her hips gently swaying, her snug-fitting jodhpurs showing her long, shapely legs to full advantage, her rounded breasts thrusting against her brightly coloured stretch top—short enough to give a tantalising glimpse of bare flesh below—it suddenly struck Taryn.

The girl wanted Mike to see the two of them working side by side, so that he'd be struck not by their similarities but by the *differences* between them! One so elegant, so sexy, so *able-bodied* and perfect…the other dishevelled and shabby after her long working day, bare-faced, her lipstick worn off, and *lame*.

Her first instinct was to get rid of Crystal on the spot. But she bit back the temptation, a defiant voice whispering that to refuse the girl's offer would be taking the easy way out. What was she afraid of? That Mike *would* make comparisons, and end up favouring the flawless Crystal? Better to put him to the test now...and find out exactly where she stood.

Besides, if she refused Crystal's help, the girl would have a perfect opportunity to moan to Mike that her generous offer had been thrown back in her face...making Taryn appear ungrateful, jealous, and fearful of the competition.

'Look,' she said, 'if you'd really like to lend a hand, come back in the morning when we exercise the horses. You can go hacking with Abby while I do some initial work with the new mare I picked up today.' There was no way she was going to let Crystal help with the real training. She knew nothing about the girl's horsemanship, and when and if she ever needed expert assistance she'd choose someone she knew and was very sure of.

If Crystal agreed to come back in the morning, she would give her one of her own older horses to exercise. The more uninteresting the girl found it, the sooner she'd get bored and leave. She didn't strike Taryn as the type to have much patience or staying power. She'd be used to more racy, glamorous pursuits.

'What, go hacking over the hills with your groom, while you stay back here at Fernlea doing all the interesting *professional* work?' Crystal gave a derisive half-smile. 'Thanks, but no, thanks.'

She paused a moment to light a cigarette, using an expensive-looking gold lighter. 'I've a better idea. It's just possible,' she said musingly, 'that I might have some work to put your way, Taryn. Well-paid work...if you'd be interested in another horse to train?'

A horse to train? Taryn hesitated. One part of her told

her to jump at the opportunity…an opportunity to train a Bannister thoroughbred and gain valuable publicity for her training centre if she did well…but another part cautioned her to think carefully before committing herself. She didn't trust this girl. Or like her. The less she saw of her the better.

She heaved a sigh as she gave Ginger's velvety nose a pat and put him away in his stall, before leading out the next horse, a big grey called Rexie.

'You don't train your own horses?' she asked the girl finally as she lifted Rexie's leg to examine his hoof.

'Not as show-jumpers…you're the expert there.' Crystal lolled against the stone wall between the timber stalls, blowing smoke rings through pursed red lips. 'I'm thinking of giving my old show mare, Glory, to a niece of mine, who's training to be a show-jumper. But the mare needs some professional training first. I'm afraid she's been out to grass and a bit neglected of late, with me away overseas. I'll bring her—' She stopped abruptly as a big grey Range Rover bounced into the yard.

Taryn raised her eyes heavenward. Oh, no, not *now*. She couldn't look at Crystal, afraid of what she might read in the girl's probing dark eyes.

'Mike!' Crystal flew to meet him as he opened his door and stepped out. Taryn stayed where she was, tending to Rexie, determined not to appear too eager by rushing to greet Mike herself. She saw Crystal glance back, as if expecting—hoping—that she would. So that she'd have the satisfaction of seeing her limping across the yard after her, knowing that Mike would be watching them…comparing them?

'Well…this seems to be a regular visiting time for you,' she heard Crystal greet Mike, her tinkling voice gently teasing rather than fractious.

'You too,' he responded dryly. 'What brings you here this time?'

'I came to tell Taryn I've some work to put her way,' Crystal said sweetly…making no mention of her offer to help with the training—or her abrupt about-turn. 'I've asked her to train my mare Glory as a show-jumper. I want to give her to my niece—a budding show-jumper—for her birthday.'

Taryn frowned. Even the most hardened male would surely melt under all that charm and sweetness and benevolence. And if Mike still had feelings for the girl…

She drew in her lips. If he couldn't see through Crystal after all this time…if he still didn't have the strength to withstand her wiles…well, he wasn't the man she'd thought he was…a man she'd want in *her* life.

And she was damned, she decided, if she was going to hide away, fearing comparisons.

She straightened, brushing some wisps of hair from her eyes. Leaving Rexie tied to a hanging loop outside the stall, she marched over to join them. In a perverse show of defiance, she made no attempt to disguise or minimise her limp as the other two turned her way.

'Hullo, Mike.' She greeted him with a brief, offhand smile as she approached. 'How's your father?'

Mike smiled at her with a warmth that put her even more off-stride. 'Coming along fine. He's off the drip and starting to give cheek. He even got out of bed today for a short time, but the rest of the day he's been flat on his back, feeling bored and frustrated. I'm sure he'd enjoy a visit from a pretty young woman…if you have the time or happen to be passing by in the next few days.'

Her heart thumped. He was asking her in front of Crystal… 'I'll go and see him tonight,' she promised, half hoping he might say he'd see her there…or even suggest going together.

'I think Smudge is going to see him tonight. Could you leave it until tomorrow? Or the next day? I have to fly up to Sydney for a few days and won't be able to visit him again myself until Friday. I'm on my way to the airport now.'

Now? 'Oh. Sure… I'd be happy to,' she said faintly, realising for the first time that he wasn't wearing his usual faded jeans and bush shirt.

Her breath caught a little as she flicked her gaze over his tan leather jacket, light-coloured shirt and smart trousers. But it wasn't the scent of the leather or the waft of aftershave that caused her breath to catch, it was the sight of *him*…the strength and maleness of him…the breathtaking physique, the vivid blue-green eyes, the tumbled hair…the hint of rough-diamond wildness.

'I must pop in to see your father myself, Mike.' Crystal's bubbly voice brought their attention back to her. 'It's been worrying me that we didn't hit it off in the past. I blame myself,' she said self-effacingly. 'I mistook his gruffness for disapproval, and reacted by pretending I didn't care…giving the false impression that I didn't like *him*.'

A second of silence followed her little speech. 'I'm not sure that would be a good idea,' Mike said finally. 'My father's not at all strong yet…and he doesn't know you're back, Crystal. Visiting him in hospital—without me—could come as too much of a shock. I don't want him getting agitated or upset.'

Taryn felt an uneasy flutter. 'Without me', he'd said. Was Mike suggesting that he would take Crystal to see his father himself, when he came back from his trip?

'I would never do anything to harm your father, Mike,' Crystal assured him. There was a ring of sincerity and warmth in her voice that caused Taryn's eyes to widen, then waver. 'I'm just so glad to hear he's coming along well.'

Mike nodded, but said no more, his face stonily impassive.

'Well, I'd better be off.' Crystal waved a lightly

tanned wrist. 'I'll bring Glory round in the morning, Taryn. I just hope you don't find her too difficult for you.' She let her gaze flutter, ever so briefly, to Taryn's right foot. 'I wouldn't want you taking on more than you can handle.' She smiled her dazzling smile, though it was Mike it was directed at now. 'It was wonderful to see you again, Mike.'

With that she swung away, almost gliding over to the red Jaguar with her hips gently—provocatively—undulating as she walked. A picture of beguiling feminine perfection, her sparkling smile and enchanting voice a lingering image.

Clever, Taryn thought with a faint twinge. Very clever. Instead of blatantly throwing herself at him, Crystal had adopted a more canny, subtle approach...tantalising Mike by gently withdrawing, leaving only haunting smiles and a sparkling memory behind.

She blew out a sigh. Mike had spoken once of his dream woman... 'A fairy-tale beauty with raven hair and stunning black eyes and a face and figure you only see in your dreams...' It described the girl perfectly. Crystal, when she cared to switch on the charm, would be any man's dream come true. A beautiful, entrancing, physically perfect enchantress.

And Mike, with his fantastic looks and tough, sexy, untamed air, was so damned attractive himself that it almost hurt to look at him.

Perfection. Both so...perfect. She swallowed hard.

'Would you have time to take a coffee break before I go?'

She jumped at the sound of Mike's voice—even though it was almost drowned out by the roar of the Jaguar's engine kicking to life. She glanced up at him, for the first time wondering why he'd come. He could have told her about his father and his trip interstate over the phone.

'There's something I need to tell you,' he added as if he'd sensed her hesitation.

Her eyelashes fluttered upwards. What would he *need* to tell her? Not *want* to tell her, but *need* to. It sounded a bit ominous.

'I guess I could,' she said cautiously. 'I'll just tell Abby.' Dino, she noted, had joined Abby in the stables, having come in from the far paddock. They'd soon be finished with his help.

When she joined him again Mike was lolling against the solid timber outdoor table where they often had lunch in the shade of the overhanging grapevine—which this year was covered in juicy grapes.

'Take a seat,' she invited, flicking a nervous tongue along her lips. 'I'll bring the coffee out here.'

'Right.' His teeth flashed in a smile. 'Take your time. I've twenty minutes or so before I have to leave.'

The warmth of his smile brought a jaunty spring to her step as she headed inside—until she realised he'd be watching her and became conscious of her limp, wondering if he was comparing her lopsided walk to Crystal's sexy, hip-swaying glide.

While she was boiling the water for their coffee, she flew into the bathroom to splash water on her face and run a brush through her hair. She was tempted to leave it loose this time, as she often did at the end of the day, but changed her mind and tied it back as it was before, not wanting Mike to think she was trying to compete with his ex-fiancée.

She wanted to accentuate the *differences* between them, not the similarities.

She sighed as she headed back to the kitchen, wishing now that she'd put on some lipstick as well. Crystal's dazzling image still haunted her. Did it haunt Mike too?

Despite his apparent resistance to his ex-fiancée's charms, she felt distinctly uneasy. He'd succumbed to her once before, and Crystal had planted some very powerful seeds this afternoon. What if they were already taking root in Mike's mind, under his show of indifference? What if it was *Crystal*—and the uncertainty of his feelings about her—that he *needed* to talk to her about?

CHAPTER TEN

BUT what Mike had to say to her had nothing to do with Crystal.

'I was right the other day, wasn't I,' he began, his voice breath-catchingly gentle, with a faintly rueful edge, 'when I said there was more to you than you'd revealed so far? There was a lot more to your father too,' came the grave admission, 'than I gave him credit for.'

She looked at him across the table with bemused eyes, wondering what was coming.

'I found a bundle of old newspapers in our barn today.' He paused to take a sip of his coffee. 'A headline caught my eye as I was gathering them up to get rid of them. I read the copy...' His eyes softened as they met hers. 'It was a glowing tribute to your father, Taryn. I was very wrong about him, wasn't I? He was a great loss to a lot of people...not just you and your mother.'

She nodded, her eyes misting. She knew the newspaper article he was referring to. Her mother had brought it into the hospital to show her, a week or so after the accident.

Mike raised a hand as her lips parted. 'No, let me finish. It praised your father's life and achievements...his community work...his kindness and generosity, especially to needy charities...something he'd never publicised during his lifetime. It mentioned his devotion to your mother...and to *you*, Taryn. There was quite a lot about you...about how the accident that killed your father had injured you too, forcing you to give up a brilliant career as one of Australia's most promising show-jumpers.'

'Mike—'

'Hush. It went on to say that your loss to show-jumping was deeply felt by everyone who knew you...that you were a real contender for the Sydney Olympic team. All your friends and team-mates spoke highly of you, both as an equestrian and as a person.'

He paused, his expression penitent. 'I never took your show-jumping seriously...did I, Taryn?' His mouth twisted in self-reproach. 'I thought it was just a spoilt rich girl's way of passing the time...of showing off in front of her equally privileged peers...leaving the *real* hard work and dedication to the pros. But you *were* a pro, Taryn. You could have gone to the top. I'm so sorry it didn't work out for you.'

His hand reached out to touch hers where her fingers were wrapped round her coffee mug. She shivered under his touch, but didn't want to draw attention to it by snatching back her hand. 'I admire the way you've over-come what could have been a serious disability, Taryn, to launch a challenging new career as a professional trainer.'

A pink glow coloured her cheeks. What *could have been* a serious disability, he'd said...as if he didn't con-sider her limp a serious disability at all.

Unlike Crystal, who never missed a chance to make her feel like a flawed, second-rate has-been. But Mike... Taryn looked down at the hand on hers and swallowed deeply. Mike had never shown any flinching away...had never once said anything to make her feel like a dis-abled, lesser human being.

'The article also mentioned your brilliant academic career—and how you'd given it away to pursue your equally brilliant equestrian career.' As she glanced up again, Mike's eyes were smiling into hers, the light in them sending a reluctant warmth through her. 'It gave a brief, glowing account of your successes at university as well as in the show ring...making the point that you're a person who would excel at anything you set your mind to, regardless of obstacles...that you possess not only brains and talent, but courage and dedication and perseverance...'

'Stop! Please!' Taryn begged, shaking her head. 'I can't take any more of this!' This time she did withdraw her hand, dropping it into her lap. It was trembling, she realised. 'You know how journalists rave on...'

'Not this one. This guy has a reputation as a meticulous, highly respected, *honest* journalist.' Mike glanced at his watch and sighed, before gulping down the rest of his coffee. 'Time I was heading for the airport. I just wanted you to know that I'm sorry for the things I said about your father, Taryn...and about you.' He stood up, his great shadow falling over her.

Thrusting out his hand—the same hand that had covered hers with its rough warmth a moment ago—he said with a quirky smile, 'Care to shake hands, to show we're still friends?'

Shake hands? She felt her heart waver, then dip. He made it sound as if they were closing a deal. Did he just want to square things with her...to erase his guilt at the way he'd treated her in the past...before he left for Sydney?

Before he moved on...out of her life?

She gave a shaky laugh. If she refused, he would think she was refusing to forgive him...that she still held a grudge against him. She couldn't let him go away thinking that.

She rose from her chair and held out her hand.

His fingers closed round it...and tightened. But instead of giving it a shake and letting it go he used his firm grip on her to pull her towards him. She gasped as he dragged her hard up against his chest, his other arm sliding round her back, crushing her against him. This time it *was* the scent of leather that brought a catch to her throat, as she found her face buried in its softness.

For a timeless second she didn't move, didn't breathe. All she was aware of in that breath-stopping moment was the wild beating of her heart—or was it his?—and the warmth and muscled strength of the man holding her. Then she felt his chest heave, heard his deep voice rumble through her.

'I must go or I'll miss my plane.' His fingers curled under her chin, tilting her face to his. For a moment, as her eyelashes fluttered upwards, she wondered at the brooding look in his eyes. Until he growled, 'I wish you hadn't agreed to train Crystal's mare...but that's your business. Just try not to get too close to her...hmm?'

He caught her face in his hands and gave her a quick, almost savage kiss on the lips. Then he released her abruptly and strode off, over to the waiting Range Rover.

She stared after him, running a moist tongue over her tingling lips. Why had he kissed her like that? Was it a goodbye kiss? A final, determined goodbye? Did he feel a bit guilty about it—about dumping her—and that brief, scorching kiss was his way of softening the blow...and salving his conscience?

Or was he simply trying to forget Crystal...to blot her dazzling image from his mind...by kissing *her*, Crystal's look-alike, in that fierce, almost desperate way?

She turned away with a heavy heart and a confused mind, not even raising a hand as he drove off.

A girl had her pride.

She was gulping down her early morning coffee after a troubled, almost sleepless night, when she heard someone drive into the yard. She hurried out, expecting to see her delivery of feed arriving, even though it normally didn't come until later in the morning.

Her jaw dropped when she saw a familiar pale green Mercedes with a horse-float behind...and Crystal stepping out of the car. It was barely seven a.m.!

She saw Crystal's gaze doing a quick sweep of the

yards and stables, as if she was looking to see who else might be there. Taryn wondered if she was looking for Mike's Range Rover...checking to make sure it wasn't there. Did the girl suspect he might have lied about having a plane to catch last night...and stayed the night here at Fernlea...with *her*?

'Ah, Taryn...there you are.' There was no smile. No charm. No warmth. Of course not... Mike wasn't watching now.

Even at this early hour, the girl looked stunning. She was wearing an electric-blue tracksuit that must surely have originated in Paris or Milan, and her face was fully made up, her lips a slash of vivid red against the glossy raven locks tumbling loose over her shoulders.

'Well, you're bright and early,' Taryn greeted her, determined to be pleasant and businesslike and treat the girl as she would any other client...though it was hard when Crystal made no attempt to move forward to meet her as she crossed the yard, but stood watching her with a sardonic gleam in her eyes...making Taryn acutely aware of her limp. The girl was enjoying feeling superior, no doubt.

'Mike get away all right last night?' she asked coolly as Taryn drew closer.

So it *was* Mike on her mind. 'As far as I know,' she answered with equal coolness. 'You've brought your mare, I take it?' *Keep it businesslike,* she thought. *Keep Mike out of it.*

Crystal's response was an impatient flick of her wrist, as if to say, Well, I'd hardly bring an empty float. She was peering into Taryn's face as if trying to read what was there. Expecting to see a bedroom glow from the night before? Signs of tears at Mike's week-long absence? Despondency at the sight of a rival? An *able-bodied* rival?

After a moment, Crystal said levelly, 'You do realise that Mike's using you to forget me. The poor dear's afraid to face up to the fact that he still has feelings for me. He's terrified of getting hurt again.' She paused, her eyes never leaving Taryn's face. 'Has he talked about our break-up at all?'

Taryn shook her head. 'Crystal—'

The red lips curved. 'No, he wouldn't…he's too much of a man. Too much of a *gentleman*.' With a roll of her hips, the girl stepped closer. 'I never left him for another man, Taryn, as a lot of people seem to think. Mike and I never even looked at anyone else…we were crazy about each other. We had a silly quarrel…over his work…and I threw back his ring in a fit of temper. I've no one to blame but myself for what happened after that…'

She bowed her head, the shining black waves swirling round her smooth cheeks. 'Mike's a proud man…not the type of man to come crawling after a girl. I was just as proud and headstrong in those days… I pretended not to care. In a terrible overreaction, I turned to someone else…and married him on the rebound. I hurt Mike terribly. I'd never hurt him again, Taryn. And I wouldn't want to see *you* get hurt, by holding out any vain hopes.'

Oh, wouldn't you just? Taryn brooded, hiding the utter devastation she was feeling inside. It rang true… everything the girl had said. She didn't want to hear any more. She could certainly do without hearing the details of their brief reunion last summer. 'Crystal, I agreed to train your mare…simply that. I don't intend to discuss your private life. Or Mike O'Malley's. Let's get to work, shall we?'

'Why not?' Crystal gave a brief, cool smile. She'd made her point, said what she'd wanted to say, and was satisfied.

A few hours later Taryn was wondering what on earth she'd taken on. Beautiful as Crystal's mare was, she was skittish, highly strung, easily upset, and disobedient. She shied for no apparent reason. She tended to nip and kick. Her temperament warned that she was likely to be an erratic, anxious jumper, difficult to train.

Glory, Taryn realised with a sigh, was going to need a lot of careful, patient handling if she hoped to turn the mare into the reliable, proficient show-jumper Crystal expected. Obedience training and confidence-building would have to be top priority to begin with, along with a good balanced diet...followed by weeks of firm, calm, regular training.

And the girl had given her just one month to have the mare trained and in peak condition for her niece's birthday!

When Taryn had argued that it would take at least eight to ten weeks in Glory's case, the girl had taunted, 'If you don't feel up to it, Taryn, I'll take her to someone who *is* capable of handling her. But it won't do your reputation—or your fledgling equestrian centre—any good.'

The veiled threat hadn't been lost on Taryn. The Bannisters, with their many contacts in the thoroughbred community, would be quite capable of ruining her reputation—and her livelihood.

'Oh, it's not that I'm not capable,' she'd returned evenly. 'I was thinking of your *mare*, Crystal...what's best for her. After such a long rest period it would be quite wrong to work her too hard too soon. Her training must be done gradually...and properly. I do know what I'm doing.'

'Four weeks,' Crystal had repeated, and left her to it— promising to come back at the end of the week to see how things were progressing.

The end of the week... *Friday*, did she mean? The day Mike was due back?

Taryn smiled grimly. Crystal was hoping, no doubt, that her mare would have made no progress by then...and that Mike would be around to witness his incompetent neighbour's dismal failure. And she didn't doubt that Crystal would put on a touching show of disappointment, before announcing with mock regret that she would have to withdraw her mare from Taryn's unsatisfactory care!

She sighed again as she turned her attention back to Glory...only to have the mare shy away, showing the whites of her eyes as she reached out to her.

Taryn's own eyes narrowed in quick suspicion. Had Crystal deliberately chosen the most difficult horse possible, to ensure that she *did* fail? Hoping to show her up as incompetent in Mike's eyes? Hoping that her sense of inadequacy and failure would discourage her enough to give up her training ambitions, sell Fernlea, and slink off...back to the city?

Well, you don't know Taryn Conway, lady. Taryn's eyes gleamed with deadly resolve. *I'm not going to fail. And I'm not going to be panicked into hounding your poor mare until she's even more of a nervous wreck than she is already, and refuses to do anything, just because you want results in a month.*

'You're going to be trained properly, Glory, my girl, and not rushed,' she said aloud—speaking gently, so as not to spook the mare. 'And you're going to be handled with the utmost care, using every skill I possess.' She ran her hand down the mare's sleek neck, stroking steadily until the flighty animal calmed down.

'And if you're not a calmer, more obedient, better behaved mare by the end of this first week, so that I can show Crystal that you're making some progress, then I *deserve* to be sacked.'

For all her fine intentions, it was a long, difficult, and at times frustrating week, though she wasn't sure if it was the antics of Crystal's mare that were making the days drag so much...or Mike's lengthy absence. She was missing him far more than she would have believed possible.

Which was very foolish of her, she knew, when he was probably thinking more of Crystal—the bewitching, perfect Crystal—than he was of *her*. Crystal's smug words still haunted her. 'The poor dear's afraid to face up to the fact that he still has feelings for me. He's terrified of getting hurt again.'

Was he? If he could weaken once…

She tried not to think about him, throwing all her energy into the needs of Crystal's mare…only attending to her other horses while Glory was resting.

She gave the mare gentle, regular handling several times a day, with just sufficient work at this early stage to improve the mare's condition and earn her trust. For the first few days she made no attempt to ride Glory, giving her some gentle lunging on a long rope instead…always talking to her in a firm, gentle voice.

When she did finally try to saddle her, the mare went wild, kicking and protesting. Taryn had seen it happen before, with horses who'd had saddles banged down on their backs and the girths done up too tightly, resulting in the animals associating saddles with discomfort.

'All right, Glory. All right, girl.' She fitted an extra-soft saddle cloth under the saddle, and used a more comfortable nylon girth, and the next time she tried, ever so gently, Glory accepted the saddle without demur.

By the time Friday arrived, she felt she'd at last earned Glory's respect…and trust. The mare had begun to respond to the calm, steady handling and to obey simple commands, and it was a very satisfying start. There was still a long way to go, of course—weeks of hard work ahead—before Glory became the show-jumper Crystal wanted her to be. The mare hadn't even started on the jumps yet. It was far too soon.

But even Crystal, Taryn fervently hoped, must see the difference in her mare, after only these few days of training. Abby and Dino were impressed with what she'd done so far. Why not Crystal?

Even so, she found she was holding her breath as Crystal's red Jaguar drove into the yard late in the afternoon, while she was tying up a haynet for Glory in the stables. The mare had already been groomed and brought in for the night.

'How are you managing?' Crystal asked, running sharp eyes over her mare, as if expecting her to be showing signs of distress or panic. When she saw neither she rapped out, 'Have you saddled her yet? Ridden her?'

'Both. No problems,' Taryn answered coolly. 'She didn't like the saddle at first, but—' She broke off as a phone shrilled from a ledge outside the stables. It was her new cordless telephone from the kitchen, which she often brought to the stables with her rather than leaving the answering machine on. It didn't have the range of a mobile phone, but since the reception down here was too poor for mobiles it was better than nothing.

'I'll get it.' Crystal spun round.

'No, it's—'

But the girl had already snatched it up.

With a grimace, Taryn finished what she was doing and stepped out to join her.

The girl was chatting away in the bubbly, sparkly way she normally reserved only for Mike.

Mike? Taryn's mouth went dry.

'Of course, it's early days yet,' she heard. 'You can't expect to see a lot of progress so soon...but Taryn's doing her best, poor thing. Ah, here she is now. I'll just put her on. See you, Mike.'

She handed the phone to Taryn...the sparkle in her eyes dying, along with a smile on her lips, as she stepped back.

'Hullo?' Taryn was acutely aware of Crystal hovering close by, making no attempt to attend to her mare, or to move out of hearing range.

'Taryn...how are you?' Mike's familiar deep voice brought shivery goosebumps to her skin. 'Everything OK?'

Did he mean with her, with Crystal's mare...or between her and Crystal? 'Just try not to get too close to her,' he'd said before he left. Did it embarrass him when they were together...the old flame and the possible new? Or was he worried that if they became too close, too friendly, it would make it harder for him to choose one above the other?

She almost laughed aloud at the notion. How could he possibly imagine they could ever be friends?

Because they were so alike, in so many ways?

She gulped in a quick breath. 'Fine,' she said cautiously, aware of Crystal's sharp ears and watchful black eyes.

'Good,' said Mike. 'I'm just about to leave Melbourne airport to come home. I spoke to Dad a moment ago...he says you've been in twice this week to see him. He thinks you're an angel, Taryn, taking the time to drive all that way to see him, when you have so much on your plate. He said the home-grown grapes you brought him were delicious.'

'Warragul's not so far away,' she said lightly. 'And I had some shopping to do there anyway. And the last time I saw him I went at night, when things are quieter. Anyway, it was a pleasure. He's coming along well, Mike.'

'Great. I'm on my way to see him now... I should be there in a couple of hours. How about meeting me at the hospital, Taryn...if you're free tonight, of course? Maybe we could have a spot of dinner after seeing him? There's a new Italian restaurant in the town, apparently.'

She snatched in a quick breath, feeling inexplicably pleased that he wanted to have dinner with her. And at a public restaurant! She'd been to few restaurants in the past year or so...and none since she'd been back at

Fernlea. She normally cooked for her mother or for any friends who came down to stay overnight.

'All right... I'd love to. It will be a pleasant change to eat out. I'll meet you at the hospital in...two hours, you said? Around seven? Right.' As she broke contact she caught Crystal's eye. There was a speculative gleam in the narrowed depths, a tightening of the shapely red lips, that caused her heart to wobble.

Crystal would have heard everything! Not just that she was meeting Mike at the hospital, but that they were having dinner together afterwards. And Mike, it occurred to her, her heart sinking further, must have known that Crystal was still there, and probably listening in!

'Mike's using you to forget me,' the girl had told her the other day.

Was he? Or was he using her to make Crystal *jealous*?

'Crystal, I'm really busy,' she said, replacing the phone on the ledge with a shaky hand. 'As you've seen, Glory is making good progress. Now, if you'll excuse me...'

'I have to go anyway.' Crystal gave a mocking half-smile, which Taryn interpreted as, Mike's not here, so why bother to stay? 'I know you must be in a rush to get your work done so you can make yourself beautiful for Mike.' She glanced down at Taryn's right foot, as if to indicate how useless the effort would be.

'Good luck, Taryn,' she threw over her shoulder as she headed back to her car, the smile still on her lips— and a pitying glint in her eye that clearly said, You'll need it.

Taryn turned away in disgust. If only Mike could see this side of his charming Crystal! But the girl would be too shrewd and cunning ever to let that happen.

And to say anything to Mike herself would only smack of sour grapes—or even malice. Which Crystal must know full well.

*   *   *

She arrived at the hospital just after seven, with a basket of fresh fruit in her hand. Mindful of Crystal's taunts, she'd deliberately—defiantly—avoided wearing any make-up other than a soft pink lipstick and a dab of powder…or dressing in anything too eye-catching, deciding on a simple white shirt and wide-legged black trousers. She'd again pulled her hair back, but this time had coiled it in a knot rather than a ponytail.

Mike was already there.

Her heart leapt at the sight of him. There was no sign of his leather jacket tonight—it was far too warm for jackets in the current heatwave, which had already lasted four days—and the pale blue sports shirt he was wearing seemed moulded to every taut, sinewy muscle, accentuating his splendid physique and powerful shoulders, while at the same time enhancing the brilliant blue-green of his eyes. His hair was as wild as ever. She suspected that no comb or brush could ever tame it for long.

She plucked her gaze away to greet Patrick, who was sitting in a chair this evening, looking pale but perky.

'Good to see you looking better, Patrick,' she said warmly.

'He's a tough old codger, isn't he?' Mike commented as she smilingly handed his father the basket of fruit she'd brought. Knowing Patrick had enjoyed the grapes she'd brought him the other day—from her own grapevine at Fernlea—she'd brought him some more, as well as some apples, pears, and some rare mulberries.

'They're from the orchard up in the pine forest,' she told him. 'Abby, Dino and I took the horses up there this morning for exercise.'

'No storms this time, I trust?' Mike murmured, and she felt herself blushing as she recalled how they'd ridden home together on her gelding, Ginger, the first time they'd met, with Mike's very masculine frame moulded to hers as closely as his shirt was moulded to him now.

'No…though I wish there had been. We badly need

some rain,' she said, changing the subject to the safety of the weather. 'The dams are low, the river's barely a trickle, and with the grass so dry and brown...' She bit the rest off, realising that Patrick was probably listening.

She could have kicked herself. The last thing she wanted to do was worry Mike's father about droughts and feeding problems while he was stuck here in hospital. She turned to him with a bright, rallying smile. 'Isn't it lucky you put in that extra dam last year? Smudge tells me your cows are thriving, Patrick.'

'Talking of Smudge,' Mike put in helpfully, 'did you know he's had a secret sweetheart all these months, and has just popped the question—and been accepted?'

'No!' She turned to him in surprise. Smudge was a man of few words, who kept his private life to himself. 'Who's the lucky girl?'

'Lucy...the girl who comes to clean our house...and yours too, I believe.'

'Really?' She couldn't believe it. Lucy—the pretty local lass who worked for several homes in the area—had never said a word, never dropped a hint. Not that Lucy was the type to gossip...least of all about her own love life. She was as shy and reticent as Smudge. 'I wonder how they ever drummed up the nerve to speak to each other,' she said with a chuckle, 'let alone court each other. When did you find out?'

Mike grinned. 'Smudge told me when I rang him from the airport...after I'd spoken to you. I asked him if they were planning to celebrate, and when he told me they'd probably just have a drink at the pub I invited them both to join us for dinner tonight. To celebrate with us. I hope you don't mind.'

'No, of course not,' she said with a bright smile, even though her heart swooped a little. So she and Mike wouldn't be alone. Did Mike prefer it that way? He'd spoken to Smudge immediately after speaking to her...and he'd spoken to Crystal before that. Had the

memory of Crystal's sparkling chatter haunted him afterwards...her warm friendliness seducing him, turning
him off the idea of an intimate dinner alone with his ex-
fiancée's not so sparkling look-alike? After all, there was
safety in numbers.

Avoiding an evening alone with his next-door neighbour would give him more time to think about what he
really wanted. Perhaps neither of them—she sighed—
because if he didn't want Crystal, surely he wouldn't
want a woman who looked so much like her?

Yes...maybe it was just as well they *weren't* going to
be alone.

'Who's celebrating what?' said a bubbly voice from
the open doorway, and a shocked silence fell over the
room as Crystal ambled in, with a large gold-wrapped
box in her arms.

She'd changed since Taryn had seen her a couple of
hours ago, and the impact of her sleeveless red sundress
and matching red sandals—with her black eyes dramatically enhanced with eye-shadow and mascara, her smiling lips a brilliant, glossy red, and her raven hair
tumbling in glossy abandon round her tanned shoulders—was breathtaking.

'Crystal...' Mike stepped between the girl and his father. He wasn't smiling, Taryn noted, but his face
seemed more resigned than angry, now that he'd recovered from his initial shock.

'I won't upset your father, Mike.' Crystal placed a
reassuring hand on his arm. 'You *did* say I could come
while you were here. And when Taryn told me she was
meeting you here at seven, well, I was sure you wouldn't
mind if I popped in too...just for a minute.'

Taryn gritted her teeth. She felt like snapping back, *I
didn't tell you...you were listening in when I spoke to
Mike!*

She met Mike's eye for a fleeting second, and caught

his brief frown. Did he think she'd been deliberately *gloating* to Crystal about meeting him here tonight?

She felt a wave of despondency as Mike steered Crystal over to his father's chair. So now he saw her as the type of woman who would gloat over a rival. Great!

Would that make him look more kindly on Crystal…and less warmly towards *her*?

'Dad, I don't think I mentioned to you that Crystal was back home.' Mike spoke up before either Crystal or his father had a chance to. 'We met the other day at Fernlea, when she and her father were visiting Taryn on business.' His tone was coolly offhand. Presumably, Taryn surmised, to calm his father and avoid any possible stress—or angry eruption. 'When she heard you were in hospital, Dad, she expressed the wish to come and see you.'

'I wanted to come earlier, Mr O'Malley, but Mike said it was too soon.' Crystal darted forward with an engaging smile. 'It's lovely to see you again, it really is! I was so terribly sorry to hear you weren't well. Are you feeling better?'

Her sickly sweet tone made Taryn feel quite ill. The girl was pulling out all the stops to charm the old man…to make him forget there had ever been any antagonism between them in the past.

'I've brought you something that I hope will cheer you up.' With a flourish, Crystal thrust the gold-wrapped box into his hands.

As Patrick frowned up at her from under grizzled brows, Crystal waved a ringless hand. 'You must be wondering why I'm back, Mr O'Malley.' She heaved a sigh. 'My marriage is over, you see. My husband let me down badly, I'm afraid…and I've come home to lick my wounds.' She threw Mike a bewitching smile. 'It was wonderful to meet up with Mike again… I didn't even know he was back in Australia.'

'I'll leave you to talk to your father, Mike,' Taryn

whispered, beginning to back away. She couldn't stand any more of this. 'I'll wait outside...' She summoned a smile as she raised a hand to his father. 'Good to see you looking better, Patrick...'

'No, wait...' Mike's voice stopped her. 'I think it's time we *all* left Dad to rest. I had a good talk to him earlier, before you came...and after all the exercises they've given him this afternoon it's time he was back in his bed.'

'Before we go...' Crystal scooped the gold-wrapped box from the old man's hands. 'Let me open this for you, Mr O'Malley...' Peeling away the gold wrapping, she looked up at him expectantly, clearly waiting for the 'oohs' and 'aahs'.

Patrick gave a snort of laughter. '"Death by Chocolate",' he read out with heavy irony. 'Very apt. Well, I suppose the nurses will lap them up.'

'Oh! Don't you like chocolates?' Crystal's lovely eyes wavered. 'They're the very best chocolate truffles that money can buy. They're imported from—'

'My father's on a special heart diet.' Mike's harsh voice sliced in. 'Chocolates are out. Not that my father's ever been a chocaholic, fortunately. Never mind, I'm sure they won't go to waste.' He caught Crystal's arm and tugged her away. 'See you, Dad. Time you were getting back into bed.' He ushered the two women out.

'Oh, Mike, I'm sorry!' As they left the ward, Crystal looked up at him with a stricken expression, appealing to him with all the magnetism of her limpid dark eyes. 'I didn't think—'

'No, you didn't. But let's forget it. At least you came. I know how you hate hospitals and sickness.'

'It was a pleasure to come and see your father, Mike.' Crystal's face brightened at the mellowing in his tone. 'You know I'd do anything for you.'

Taryn wrinkled her nose. So Crystal hadn't come to the hospital out of concern for Patrick. She'd just wanted to score marks with Mike. She'd nearly blown it with her thoughtless gift, but Mike had forgiven her. No doubt thinking she'd made her expensive purchase with good intentions.

Her own modest gift had cost nothing. A few grapes from her own grapevine, and some fruit from an old, neglected orchard up in the forest. It seemed a paltry offering by comparison. Even if a healthier one!

'What are you doing about dinner, Mike?' Crystal was asking ingenuously. 'Why don't we have dinner here in town? I mean...we have to eat, don't we?' She was gazing up at Mike with dark, beguiling eyes. Excluding Taryn. Hoping, no doubt, that her tedious rival would obligingly make some excuse to slink away.

Mike seemed to hesitate. 'Sorry, Crystal...we're meeting friends. You don't know them,' he said curtly. By now they'd reached the hospital car park, and Crystal's red Jaguar was the first car they reached. Parked in an area reserved for doctors only, Taryn noted. 'Goodnight, Crystal,' Mike said firmly.

Taryn held her breath as she waited for the girl's re-action. She was amazed when Crystal took the rebuff in her stride, flashed a brilliant smile, and trilled, 'Bye, Mike. Enjoy your dinner.'

She flicked a glance at Taryn as she swung towards her car. 'I'll see you soon, Taryn. Perhaps you'll have more luck with my mare this coming week... I do hope so. I'll pop round to check on her in a day or so.'

Their eyes met for a fleeting second and Taryn re-coiled at the stark malignancy in the black eyes before they snapped away.

But Mike had already turned away, and saw nothing.

CHAPTER ELEVEN

TARYN had a smile on her lips as she drove home, with Mike's Range Rover following her for most of the way, until the road branched into two and she veered off to Fernlea. She saw Mike's headlights swing the other way.

It was very late. The four of them had stayed at the restaurant for hours, drinking strong coffee and talking.

She'd enjoyed her evening far more than she'd expected to. Whether it was Crystal's absence...or Mike's presence...or the general *bonhomie* of the occasion...

She smiled. All three, probably. All she knew was that she hadn't had so much fun—hadn't laughed as much—for a long time. Even the normally reticent Smudge and shy little Lucy had revealed a more lively, garrulous side, after a champagne or two. The couple were obviously in love and ecstatically happy.

Mike had seemed determined to make this a special occasion for them. When he heard that Smudge hadn't had time yet to buy Lucy a ring, he'd insisted that they both have the next day off to go shopping. She'd seen him hand Smudge what looked like a cheque, and had overheard him murmur, 'Buy yourselves an engagement present...or put it towards the ring.'

Mike had topped off the evening with further good news for the happy couple. 'Thanks to Taryn's generosity you, young Lucy, won't have to live in Smudge's cramped bungalow off Dad's house...which may be all right for a bachelor, but certainly not for a newly married couple. You'll have your own house to live in, now that we've bought Plane Tree Flats. You'll be moving into the old house, where Dino and Abby were living until just recently. So...let's drink to Taryn this time, shall we?'

His eyes had met hers over their raised glasses, and she'd almost fainted under the impact of those incredible eyes of his...their glittering warmth whirling her back to the first time they'd met, when she'd opened her eyes in the forest to find herself drowning in what had seemed like a tropical blue-green sea.

She was still smiling as she swung the Land Cruiser through Fernlea's gates.

The phone started ringing as she stepped into the house. She snatched it up, knowing it would be Mike. Even though she'd told him it wasn't necessary, he'd insisted that he was going to call her, to make sure she'd reached home safely.

'Hi!' she said brightly, her mind conjuring up his face as she waited for him to speak...expecting an equally cheery 'hi!' from him.

'Good...you're home safe and sound.' There was something in Mike's voice that didn't sound quite right. It lacked the buoyancy and warmth she'd been expecting. She would have sworn there was a faint guardedness...a reticence...*something*. 'Sleep tight, Taryn.'

As she opened her mouth to answer, she heard another voice. A *woman's* voice.

'Mike, where *are* you?'

It was a voice she recognised.

Crystal's voice.

And then the phone went dead.

Taryn stood for a long, frozen moment, her heart chilled to the bone. *Crystal* was there...at Mike's. She must have been waiting there for him. And he'd invited her in!

Or had she already been *in* the house? By prior arrangement?

Had Mike given her a key?

She stopped breathing, a sudden, terrible suspicion

growing in her mind. Had Mike's cold hostility to Crystal been nothing but an act all along? Had his initial stony resistance to his ex-fiancée dissolved the moment she'd reappeared in his life—as it had dissolved once before—and he'd just kept up the pretence that he didn't care about her for his own self-preservation? Or pride or whatever?

Or had he actually given in to his feelings *days* ago, before he'd even gone away? And revealed his true feelings to Crystal *then*?

All colour drained from her face. Had the two of them been playing some insidious, brilliantly clever game ever since? In an attempt to discourage her…demoralise her…pervade her with enough self-doubt to make her scrap her ambitious plans for Fernlea and return to the city?

She clutched her chest, gulping in quick, painful breaths. Had Mike—with Crystal's full knowledge—kept up the pretence that he was still harshly bitter towards his ex-fiancée, knowing it would make a brilliant smokescreen to cover what he really wanted? What they both wanted?

Fernlea?

She staggered to a chair and slumped into the soft cushions. No! She couldn't believe such a thing of Mike. He'd always done his best to build up her esteem, not to shatter it, the way Crystal so delighted in doing. And apart from that one brief lapse with his ex-fiancée early last summer he'd always appeared so honourable and trustworthy. So honest and genuine.

But if Mike had never stopped loving Crystal…if he'd secretly yearned for her all this time, despite what she'd done to him in the past, how tempting it must have been to find that she was back home, and available again. Not only available, but *offering* herself to him. As a free woman this time.

She groaned aloud. The way Crystal had been throwing herself at him, using every feminine wile in the book, it was little wonder Mike hadn't been able to withstand her. What man could?

Oh, Mike, is it true? Despite Crystal's presence in his house tonight, she still didn't want to believe it.

But niggling memories kept taunting her, adding to the weight against him.

His kiss the other night had been savagely abrupt, as if his conscience—a sense of guilt, perhaps—had been bothering him. And tonight he'd chosen not to be alone with her. He'd organised a foursome for dinner, and had asked her to meet him at the hospital rather than picking her up from Fernlea—which had meant he hadn't had to drive her home afterwards.

Added to that, he'd been away all week...

Crystal had been away all week too.

Her heart gave a sickening wrench. Had his ex-fiancée gone to Sydney with him? Or met him somewhere, after he'd finished his business interstate?

She buried her face in her hands. She had to find out! She had to know for sure...these doubts were driving her mad.

Tomorrow... She would confront Mike tomorrow. She would drive over first thing in the morning and find out once and for all. Even if he laughed in her face for being such a gullible little fool. Even if he and Crystal *both* laughed at her. They could hardly deny being involved if they were both still there at his house together...*having spent the night together.*

She quailed at the thought of finding them both there...shrinking at the prospect of facing the two of them...seeing their reaction...seeing their faces confirming their guilt.

If they *were* guilty. If they weren't...if Crystal's presence there tonight was entirely innocent...

How shaming it would be. No...she couldn't do it! No way could she do it! She would wait until she met up with Mike again—whenever that might be—and ask him, calmly and non-accusingly, to explain why Crystal had been there.

Meantime, she simply had to get some sleep. She was worn out...drained physically and emotionally. If she could just drag herself to bed...

She *had* to.

The phone beside her bed woke her. She opened a bleary eye...blinking into the pearly light flooding in through the window. As she reached out groggily, she squinted at her clock radio.

Eight o'clock!

Her eyes snapped wide open. It was impossible! She never slept in this late! Not that she'd had much sleep. Barely any. Despite her crushing weariness, she'd tossed and turned for most of the night. She must have finally dropped off out of sheer exhaustion.

'Hullo,' she mumbled into the phone.

'Good morning.'

It was Mike's voice!

It sounded more normal this time, the guarded note of last night gone. 'How about coming over for a bite of lunch later?' he invited. 'There's something I want to tell you.'

That he was sick of the pretence, and wanted to tell her about Crystal? That they were getting back together? Her heart shrivelled inside her.

He went on, but she barely heard, despair washing over her, her mind a grey fog. 'You could ride over, Taryn... The river's so dry you'll be able to cross it anywhere. It'll be quicker than driving the long way round by road, or even cutting through Plane Tree Flats. But be careful...there's a ferocious wind blowing. Be careful of falling branches.'

'All right,' she agreed dully, conscious for the first time of the rattling windows, the rustling trees, the whine of the wind. When she glanced towards the window, she saw that the pearly glow was actually a grey blanket of cloud. As grey as her mood.

'I must fly,' Mike said cheerfully. 'I want to check on a cow that's about to calf down on Plane Tree Flats.' He'd told her over dinner last night that he'd moved some pregnant cows and calves down there. 'Bye for now.' The phone went dead.

'There's something I want to tell you...' The words thudded over and over in her head, bringing an aching tightness. So she was finally going to know...but only, she suspected, because Crystal had given the game away by opening her mouth last night while Mike was on the phone to her.

Sighing, she dragged herself to the bathroom. Not having to meet him until lunchtime gave her the whole morning to prepare for what was coming...to compose herself enough to face him...and pretend it didn't matter. Or was Mike hoping—were he and Crystal both hoping—that it *would* matter? That it would matter so much that she would decide to give up Fernlea in despair...opening the way for them to buy the property once she'd gone?

But she couldn't dwell on any of that now! She had work to do. And the first thing she must do was apologise to Abby and Dino for sleeping in!

Not bothering with breakfast, or even coffee, she threw on a shirt and a pair of old jeans, tied back her hair and flew outside. The wind, a hot westerly, was even stronger now, roaring through the trees, tearing off leafy twigs and branches, sending any loose debris flying. As the morning went on it began to become a real worry. High winds in summer, with tinder dry hills, were always a worry. Bushfires were the main concern, but falling trees or heavy branches could also cause serious trouble.

To make her morning even worse, a pale silver-green Mercedes drove into the yard, towing a horse-float.

Her stomach clenched as Crystal emerged from the driver's seat, looking as stunning as ever in a canary-yellow sundress, her glossy black hair flying in the wind.

'I've decided to give my mare to someone else to train.' The girl spoke brusquely, not bothering with a greeting. 'I'm not satisfied with Glory's progress.'

Taryn opened her mouth to argue that she'd barely had the mare a week, but she shut it again. Why bother? Crystal's mind was obviously made up, and the sooner the girl was out of her life the better. The reason behind Crystal's sudden about-face was obvious. The pretence was over. Now that the girl was confident she'd won— now that she and Mike had apparently reconciled—it was understandable that she'd want to withdraw her mare and sever all ties with the woman Mike had shown an interest in.

'Would you fetch Glory, please?' Crystal commanded.

'Certainly,' Taryn said shortly. Crystal was hoping, no doubt, that this blow to her professional pride—coming on top of losing Mike—would be the last straw.

Well, she was mistaken. She thrust out a defiant jaw. If Crystal and Mike thought she was going to sell up and go—if they thought she was going to let Fernlea fall into *their* hands—they didn't know Taryn Conway. She wasn't. She loved her life down here in South Gippsland, and despite losing the mare, despite losing Mike, she was excited at the prospect of her new equestrian centre and determined to succeed. There was no way she was going to run away...or be driven away.

Somehow she would face Mike O'Malley at lunch-time and not show, by so much as a flicker, how devastated she really was. She still had to live next door to the O'Malleys. If Mike and Crystal didn't like it, let *them* find another property. She was sure Crystal's doting father, Curtis Bannister, would be only too happy to help them.

A little later she popped back to the house to make sure that all the windows were shut in the unlikely event of rain, and to check her answering machine.

She was surprised to find a message from Mike.

'Lunch is off, I'm afraid.' No pleasant greeting this time. His tone held a clipped urgency. 'I've some trouble here. The pregnant cow I went to check on is caught in the fence down on the flats...the wires are badly twisted round her legs. I've come back for the pliers and wire-cutters...it's going to take me some time. She's our best cow, and she's carrying a valuable calf... I'll have to be very careful. And after I've dealt with the cow I'll have to fix the fence. Be in touch later.'

Taryn swallowed as she reset the machine. Although her heart went out to the pregnant cow, she was relieved that her lunch with Mike was off. It meant that she could imagine for a little longer that she might have been mistaken about Mike and Crystal...that Mike just might have an acceptable excuse for having his ex-fiancée at his house last night...that he might still be the man she respected and...

She groaned. Loved. *Yes...admit it, you poor fool. You love him. You've been in love with him from the moment you first met him up in the pine forest, when he kissed you and you nearly drowned in those incredible eyes of his...*

'Taryn! *Taryn!* Where are you?'

Her head whipped round. Abby appeared breathlessly at the kitchen door. 'I can smell smoke!' she gasped. 'I can't see anything from the yard; those big cypresses and oaks are in the way. I'm going round the front of the house to—'

'I'll come with you!'

She smelt it too, the moment she plunged out of the

door. The vicious wind tore at them as they ran, the smoke-filled air pungent in their nostrils, their eyes smarting.

A moment later they pulled up in horror. Just up the road, in dense bush at the base of the next hill, they saw billowing smoke, a lethal red glow, and roaring flames licking high into the air.

'Oh, my God…it's bad!' Taryn croaked. The bushfire was in the worst possible spot…in an area thick with blackwoods, wattles and gum trees…all tinder-dry and dangerously volatile.

And the wind—her blood chilled in her veins—was blowing the blaze directly towards Fernlea! Driven on by the force of the wind, with dry grass and thick bush in its path, there would be nothing to stop it!

She grabbed Abby's arm. 'Find Dino and bring all the horses in…quick! We haven't much time.' There wouldn't be time to call the CFA. No point either…it would take them a good hour to rally volunteers and then reach the fire. An hour would be too late!

Hair lashed into her eyes and she clawed it away. 'I'll start hosing down the house and the gutters!' she shouted as they both broke into a run. 'The stables should be OK, with the bare yard in between the barn and the fire, but get Dino to hose them down all the same.'

She knew that in ferocious winds like today's anything could happen. She'd heard of fires jumping entire hills. Even a mere spark could be dangerous…it could leap far ahead of the fire.

In the next fifteen minutes or so they all worked frantically, aware that the fire was terrifyingly close, and advancing at a frightening rate. Heavy smoke and ash swirled round them, making them blink and cough. They knew, despairingly, that even trained fire-fighters would have little chance of stopping the blaze in these appalling conditions.

'I can't lose Fernlea…I can't!' Taryn gasped, knowing that her feeble attempts to save her house, by filling the gutters with water and hosing down the roof and walls and the shrubs closest to the house, would be in vain if the fire reached the big old trees bordering the homestead. These gale-force winds would sweep the flames across to the house without even touching the parched lawn in between. She'd be lucky to escape to safety herself.

It dawned on her a moment later that something had changed...that her hair was being whipped a different way...that the ominous wall of smoke and flames, clearly visible now from the house, was veering away...*away from Fernlea*.

The wind had changed direction!

She waited a few minutes to make sure, then dropped the hose in the garden and flew to the stables, shouting to Abby and Dino, 'The wind's changed! The fire's already swung round...it's heading down the pass now, along the river, *away* from us! I think we're going to be OK!'

Her hands flew to her cheeks, all the colour draining from her face. 'Oh, no!'

Mike was down in the pass...trying to save his pregnant cow down on Plane Tree Flats! It was possible that he mightn't even know the fire was coming. If he was concentrating hard enough on what he was doing, on saving the cow and her precious calf, he mightn't even have smelt any smoke to warn him there was a fire!

'Mike's down on Plane Tree Flats!' she burst out. 'I must go and warn him!' She had no time to waste if she hoped to reach him in time.

She noticed that one of the horses—a bay gelding called Pirate—was still saddled, in readiness for a ride Abby had planned earlier, before she'd smelt smoke. Taryn grabbed the reins and sprang onto the horse's back, knowing it would be quicker to ride to the flats than to waste time finding the keys to the Land Cruiser and opening up the garage to bring it out.

'Keep the hoses on…just in case!' she instructed Abby and Dino before charging off. 'And call the CFA!' There'd been no time to do it before.

The wind was blowing from the north now, tearing at her hair and shirt as she urged Pirate across the golden-brown plateau, then down the slope towards the river. With such a force behind it, the bushfire would shoot down the tree-lined pass in no time.

She groaned aloud, the wind snatching the sound away.

The sky was low and dark, as if a storm was on its way. She prayed that it would bring rain…prayed it wouldn't be simply a dry electrical storm like the ones they'd been having lately, bringing lightning strikes without any rain, and making things a thousand times worse!

Up ahead, over to the right, she could see the smoke from the bushfire in the valley, being swept along by the tearing wind. It was advancing at an ominous rate towards Plane Tree Flats. She groaned again, fearing that Mike, intent on his pregnant cow and the broken fence, wouldn't even be aware that it was coming.

Even if the CFA were already on their way, they'd have no hope of stopping the fire in these horrendous winds. Nothing could!

With a choked cry she thought of Fernlea, still possibly in danger, despite the wind change. She knew that a bushfire, if powerful enough, could create its own wind to drive it along. What if an arm of the original front was still advancing under its own searing force? What if it was even now threatening her home?

She shuddered, momentarily closing her eyes. But she mustn't think about Fernlea. *Mike* was in danger!

She raked hair out of her eyes—her ponytail had long since come unravelled—and let out a sob of relief as she caught sight of the two giant plane trees ahead, flanking the concrete bridge leading to Plane Tree Flats.

Across the river, a short distance to the right of the bridge, was the fence that ran across the river flats to the hill behind. And there—thank God!—was Mike! He was working on the fence, his broad-shouldered frame hunched over…a picture of total concentration, his back to the danger racing towards him, his hair flying in the wind. He must have already freed the pregnant cow, which was nowhere in sight. Or any of his other cows or calves either. They must have sensed the danger and moved up over the hill out of harm's way.

'*Mike!*' she screamed as Pirate thundered towards the spot where Mike was working. 'Mike! *Fire!* Get out of there! *Now!*' The wind whipped her shouts away, but she kept on yelling. 'Mike! *Fire!* Go! Go *now*! *Mi-i-ke!*'

Finally he heard her and raised his head. Still shrieking at him, she slid from the saddle and ran the last few paces, dragging Pirate behind, her hand firmly clutching the reins.

'Mike! You have to get away from here! There's a bushfire coming! It's racing along the river, heading straight for us!'

Mike was already on his feet, his head jerking round. '*Hell!*' He'd seen it now…the smoke, the fiery glow, the licking flames. The danger.

His eyes snapped back to her. 'Let's get out of here! Go back the way you came… I'll follow you!' He ran to the motorbike he'd brought to the flats with him. 'Off you go, Taryn…*now*!'

She leapt back into the saddle…but hesitated a moment before galloping off. She wanted to make sure that Mike's motorbike started…knowing that if it didn't Pirate would have to carry both of them.

Despite the fearsome threat headed their way, an image flashed into her mind of the two of them making their escape together, Mike seated close behind her, his arms wrapped round her, the way he'd sat behind her on Ginger last summer, after his own horse, Caesar, had bolted in the storm.

'Do you notice anything?' Mike said suddenly as he was about to kick-start the motorbike's engine. His voice sounded clearer than before. 'The wind's dropped.'

She glanced up at the trees, her heart leaping. It had! The branches—the air—had suddenly become dead still...as still as the silent pine forest way up on the far hill. The only sound—they could hear it clearly now—was the crackle of the approaching fire, the roar of the flames. Would this drop in the wind slow its progress?

Something splashed in her eye. She felt another watery splash. Then another. Huge drops. She glanced at Mike, hope flaring in her eyes. The drops increased...one after the other, multiplying rapidly until they were streaming down her face and neck and thudding into the dry grass.

'Rain!' she cried joyously, lifting her face to the sky. 'Oh, Mike...do you think it will—?'

And then the heavens opened...a thunderous downpour that drenched them both and drowned out every other sound, even the sound of the bushfire.

'Go!' Mike bellowed over the din. 'Don't stop until you reach Fernlea!' But this time there was elation, not urgency in his voice. 'I'll skirt round above the river to check on the fire. This should soon put it out.'

As she hesitated again—could there still be danger from the fire?—he snapped a sharp look up at her, squinting against the pelting rain. 'Fernlea *is* all right...isn't it?'

Was it? A tiny stab of fear shot through her. With the wind and the blaze so unpredictable, there was no knowing what might have happened in her absence.

'I...think so.' She gave an uncertain wobble of her head...at the same time relishing the sensation of the rain soaking into her. It was also pouring down on the fire, soaking away the flames, soaking away the danger. 'The fire was almost on top of us, and then the wind changed,' she shouted over the rain. 'When I saw the smoke and flames veering away, heading down the pass towards Plane Tree Flats...'

'You rushed off to warn *me*,' he finished for her. '*You risked your life to save me.* Knowing that Fernlea could still be in danger. Knowing that you'd be heading into the fire's path. Knowing it could be on top of both of us by the time you reached me.'

She shook her head. 'Don't be silly, anyone would have—'

'Anyone would *not* have,' he cut in. 'Come on...let's make sure Fernlea's all right. I'll check on the fire later... Off you go! I'll follow.'

She swallowed a lump in her throat. He wanted to check on Fernlea before worrying about what the fire might have done to his own property. Before checking that the fire was out. Was he thinking of *her*? Or of a property that might one day be his? She gave herself a shake—she mustn't think about any of that now—and swung Pirate around, back the way they'd come. Mike's motorbike roared to life behind her.

Minutes later she gave a thumbs-up sign as she saw Fernlea ahead, standing safe and sound, the way she'd left it. None of the huge old English oaks or cypresses appeared to have been touched by the fire. The show-jumping course and training tracks lay intact, under sheets of water. And the horses, she found as she rode into the yard ahead of Mike, were all safely under cover, in the untouched stables.

They'd been very lucky. All of them.

And the rain was still thudding down, soaking into the parched hills and quenching, hopefully, whatever remained of the fire.

There was no sign of Abby or Dino, but their old ute had gone from the yard. She guessed they'd gone up the road to see what damage the bushfire had done, now that the danger had passed.

Mike, knowing she'd want to check for herself, waved her on.

'I'll come too,' he shouted, revving his motorbike as Pirate took off. 'I'd like to know how this fire started.'

She'd been wondering about that too. There'd been no lightning ahead of the rainstorm. No sun to scorch the earth. No one would have been burning off in gale-force winds like today's. And besides, the fire had started on her own property. No one had been anywhere near the thick scrub where the fire had started.

They came to a halt further up the road, falling silent when they saw what the bushfire had done. It wasn't a pretty sight. The charred trees and the blackened, smouldering path which the fire had left behind—and the burnt, pungent smell rising from the scorched earth and trees—caused Taryn's throat to constrict. It could have been Fernlea!

Even worse...*Mike* could have been caught in the inferno!

She shuddered, partly in horror, partly in relief. It hardly mattered, in that moment, that she had lost him to Crystal. The important thing was that he was all right. He was safe.

They saw Dino's ute up ahead, and found Abby and Dino standing among the charred wattles and black-woods where the fire had started, talking with another of Taryn's neighbours...a walnut farmer called Ted, whose property backed onto the hill rising behind.

Abby rushed up to them. 'The fire-trucks arrived a few minutes ago. They're down in the pass, mopping up. It could have been a lot worse,' she consoled Taryn.

'I know,' Taryn said fervently. 'We've been very lucky.'

'Ted's pretty sure how the fire started,' Dino put in, grim-faced. 'Tell 'em, Ted.'

'Right. I was up on the hill, clearing away some black-berries along that ridge up there...' Ted pointed '...and I saw a car pull up down below and a woman get out. She threw something over the fence...into the dry grass under these wattles and blackwoods right here. They were real bushy before...growing in a great thick clump.'

He paused dramatically. 'It must have been a match or a lighted cigarette! What else could it have been?'

'What time was this?' Mike rasped from behind.

'Just before the fire started.' Ted shrugged, looking contrite. 'I didn't think anything of it at the time—it could have been an apple-core she threw, or some bread for the birds or anything—until I saw smoke rising from that very same spot, minutes after she drove off. Then flames started leaping into the air, fanned by the wind. I knew I'd have no hope of stopping the fire by myself, barehanded...it was spreading like crazy in that fiendish wind. I knew I'd have to rush back home and call for help.'

'But Ted's son had taken their ute to another part of the property, so he was on foot.' Dino took up the story. 'Ted had to run all the way back home to call the CFA...wasting valuable time.'

'I called Fernlea too,' Ted asserted, 'but I only got your answering machine. Luckily, the wind changed pretty soon after that.' He lifted a balled fist. 'I'd like to get my hands on that woman! You could have been burnt out. We all could have.'

'What sort of car was it?' Mike rapped out. 'Did you recognise it? Or the woman?'

Ted shook his head. 'I'm not often over this side of my property... I usually don't see who drives in or out of Fernlea. I only know it was a big pale green sedan—a Mercedes, I think—and it was pulling a horse-float. And the lady was wearing a bright yellow dress.'

'Crystal Bannister!' Abby burst out, her eyes widening in shock. 'She was here earlier to pick up her mare. She was driving a pale green Mercedes and wearing a yellow sundress. And she does smoke... I've seen her.'

Crystal! *Crystal* had started the fire? *Deliberately* started it? Taryn's eyes flew to Mike's. She saw the shock in his face, the disbelief.

'Crystal.' The name grated from his lips. 'My God... I don't believe it!'

Taryn's heart wrenched at the sight of his apparent distress. *Distress* rather than anger. In an instinctive gesture of comfort she reached out to him, her fingers brushing his bare arm.

'Mike... I'm so sorry,' she breathed, her heart going out to him...even as it cracked into tiny pieces. Poor Mike... To find out that the woman he loved was capable of doing such an appalling thing...capable of deliberately throwing a lighted match or cigarette into the tinder-dry bush in the middle of summer, on a day of ripping gale-force winds!

But *why*? Why had she done it? She must have known the wind would drive the fire directly onto Fernlea... directly towards the house.

Taryn shook her head. It didn't make sense! Why would Crystal want to destroy the very house she wanted for herself? And for Mike?

Unless she hadn't meant any harm to the house at all. Unless she'd simply wanted to give Fernlea's owner a nasty fright...hoping it would knock the fight out of her and send her scampering back to the city.

Only Crystal had misjudged the wind...the force of the wind. The force of the fire. It was pure luck—the change of wind—that had saved Fernlea.

'Mike, I'm sure that if Crystal did start the fire,' she ventured huskily, 'she meant no real harm.' She hated to think of Mike being hurt again...feeling betrayed again...even if in a different way this time. Not another man...but his faith in Crystal herself. She'd done this crazy, irresponsible thing just as he was beginning to trust her again. And it was serious. To deliberately start a bushfire was a *crime*... She could be sent to gaol for it!

'She would never have meant *you* any harm, Mike, and you were in as much danger as...as we were here at Fernlea.'

'She didn't know the wind was going to change,' Mike ground out. 'When she started the fire, the wind was blowing towards Fernlea.'

It tore her in two to see the torment in his eyes. 'I'm sure she only meant to give me a bit of a scare, Mike, so that—so that I'd think twice about staying at Fernlea. But the wind was much stronger than she thought. It swept the fire out of control...

The rain, she realised, had eased to a steady sprinkle. She didn't have to shout any more. 'Mike...' She moved closer, dropping her voice. 'If you and Crystal really want Fernlea so much,' she breathed, 'you can have it. I'll find another property. There are plenty of other locations suitable for training horses...'

She couldn't go on living next door to the O'Malleys now anyway...not after this. Even if Mike and Crystal chose to live elsewhere, Mike's *father* would still be there. And Mike and Crystal would come to visit him...they might even decide to build a house on Plane Tree Flats...and she might bump into them one day.

The further away she was the better...if she ever wanted any peace of mind again.

She saw Mike's expression change to one of baffled exasperation. He caught her by both arms, his fingers gripping her so tightly she almost cried out. 'What on earth are you talking about? *If Crystal and I really want Fernlea?* What's *that* supposed to mean?'

'I—I thought—' She bit her lip, and glanced round, remembering that Dino, Abby and Ted were still within earshot. 'Forget it, Mike,' she mumbled. This was hardly the time or the place. 'Would you let me go, please?'

'You're right.' Mike dropped his hands. 'This isn't the time.'

Ted stepped forward, frowning at Mike. 'Are you going to report this woman to the police, Mike? I mean, if she's a friend of yours...'

Mike's head snapped round, his face darkening. 'Have you told anyone else about what you saw, Ted? The fire-fighters? Anyone?'

Ted shook his head. 'Not yet... Only Dino and Abby here. I haven't spoken to the fire-fighters... I only just came. I've been at home, protecting my house.'

'Good,' Mike growled. He raked a hand through his wet tangle of hair, sending tiny droplets flying. 'Look... I'd like Crystal's part in this to be kept quiet for the time being... All right? Let me handle it... Taryn and me. The damage is confined to our two properties; it's up to us to decide whether we want to bring in the police or lay any charges. I'd like to speak to Crystal first. Any objections?' He flicked a look from Ted to Abby and Dino, and waited until they shook their heads. 'No? Good!'

He swung back to face Taryn. 'I'm going home to check that Dad's cows are OK, and to see to the milking... Smudge won't be home until later tonight. He has the day off, remember? After that I'll be going over to the Bannisters' to speak to Crystal...' His eyes clouded. 'I'm sure she'll be there. I'll go home this way—' he waved a hand towards the scorched pass '—and have a word with the fire-fighters on the way, to make sure there are no danger spots left.'

He slid a hand over Taryn's shoulder, and she shivered under his touch, tempted to push his hand away— if he only knew what it was doing to her!—but she couldn't move.

She gazed bravely up at him. 'Don't be too hard on

her, Mike,' she heard herself pleading with him. 'If she did do this—this crazy thing, she would have done it because—because she loves you. Because she wanted Fernlea for *you*. She—she just wasn't thinking straight.' She gulped. What woman *could* think straight, around Mike O'Malley?

Something dark and almost frightening flared in his eyes. 'Oh, I think she knew precisely what she was doing,' he scraped out with grinding harshness. 'It was revenge...pure revenge.' His hand slipped away. 'I'll see you later, Taryn...tonight. I'll be back tonight. You'll be home?'

She nodded dazedly, staring after him with mystified eyes. *What did he mean by* revenge? And why was he coming back to see her tonight? Simply to report on his confrontation with Crystal? So that he could plead for her understanding...and for her silence, as he'd just done with the others?

CHAPTER TWELVE

TARYN wasn't sure how she survived the next few hours, waiting for Mike to come back. Revenge, Mike had said. Why would Crystal want *revenge*?

To hit back at her for setting sights on Mike? For trying to steal her man? What better revenge than to destroy her rival's beloved Fernlea? Too bad if it destroyed the property Mike wanted at the same time. Crystal had no love for the place herself.

Taryn shook her head as the questions swirled through her. Would Mike forgive Crystal for what she'd done? If he loved her enough, he might. He *would*.

Wouldn't he?

A sigh shuddered through her. Poor, deluded Mike. She couldn't believe he could be so taken in by that sweet-faced witch!

She tried to put both of them out of her mind as she threw all her energy into doing what most needed to be done, but it was near impossible. Abby and Dino made a couple of tentative attempts to engage her in conversation, but they soon gave up, realising her mind was elsewhere.

It was still raining, off and on—brief heavy downpours that soaked into the parched earth and helped to bring some relief to the dams—but she couldn't rejoice yet. She was too worried and uncertain about Mike.

At long last dusk fell and she was able to bid Abby and Dino goodnight and escape into the house...the house she could so easily have lost. She had a long steamy-hot shower, glad to get out of her damp clothes and wash the smoke and grit from her hair.

Afterwards she realised she was hungry—she'd skipped breakfast, then missed out on lunch—and set about heating some left-over soup and making herself some toasted sandwiches, not feeling up to cooking a hot meal.

There was still no sign of Mike, no call from him. Had he decided not to come? Had he decided to stay with Crystal?

Just as she was beginning to give him up altogether and sink into black despair, she heard a car drive into the yard. She didn't rush out. Pride kept her in her armchair in the den. If it was Mike, let him come to the door and knock. She wasn't going to make a fool of herself by eagerly rushing to meet him!

She heard his raised voice—'*Taryn!* Are you in there?'—and a loud banging on the kitchen door.

She swallowed, her heart leaping into her mouth. This was it. All her questions—doubts—confusions—would be resolved in the next few minutes.

Even so, she didn't hurry to the kitchen, suddenly afraid of what she might hear. Crystal was so clever...so bewitchingly, wickedly clever. She'd cast spells before...she could have cast them again, given a logical excuse for stopping the car up the road, or even denied everything and made Mike believe her.

As she opened the door Mike almost burst through the gap. She stepped back, her lips parting...and felt her right foot rolling over onto its side, her leg threatening to buckle beneath her.

As her face twisted in pain, Mike caught her, sweeping her up in his arms. 'You've hurt your foot!'

'No, I... It's fine...really,' she croaked, marvelling at the gentleness of the powerful arms holding her... cradling her as if she were no heavier than a child. 'I was just clumsy... I—I stepped back too quickly.' She was breathing too hard, too quickly, her heart banging in her chest. She hoped he couldn't feel it.

'You must have tired your foot with all that riding you did today…coming to warn *me*,' Mike muttered, striding through to the den, taking care as he carried her through the open doorway.

She shook her head…though all she really wanted to do was bury her face in his shirt. She breathed in deeply, drinking in the heady maleness of him…then expelling her breath in a bittersweet sigh.

'I haven't noticed it all day,' she asserted, and it was true…she hadn't. It was only now, after rolling over on her bad foot, that she realised her frantic ride probably *had* weakened it. The doctors had warned her that vigorous riding or overuse could do that…and that only time and rest would strengthen it.

'Funny you should say that,' Mike said, smiling down at her, the smile intensifying the lines in his deeply tanned face. '*I* noticed that when you jumped off your horse and ran to me, down on Plane Tree Flats, there was no sign at all of your limp!'

Her eyelashes flickered. 'There…wasn't?'

'Nope.' The eyes above hers burned with a glowing softness. 'You must have been thinking about something else…or some*one* else.' His voice washed over her…deep, gentle, unusually husky. 'When you're not conscious of it, it's barely noticeable…do you realise that? When you *are*, you tend to favour your other foot, putting all your weight there—maybe subconsciously trying to save your injured foot—and accentuating a limp that's barely noticeable otherwise.'

He dropped a kiss on her brow. 'You don't need to be conscious of it when I'm around, my sweetest, bravest girl… I love you just as you are…any way you are.'

A tremor shook her. *Love* you? He didn't mean that literally, of course…it was just a figure of speech, a turn of phrase, to make her feel better. *Like*, he meant.

'You—you can put me down now,' she jerked out, realising they were in the den now, surrounded by armchairs and sofas. There was no reason for him still to be holding her.

'I don't want to put you down...ever,' he growled, and she blinked up at him, her tongue flicking over her lips. 'I'm going to keep you right here where you belong...in my arms.' Still cradling her securely against his chest, he eased himself down on the nearest sofa.

She felt her heart skittering in her chest as he began to stroke her hair back from her brow with feather-light fingers, his incredible blue-green eyes glowing with a tenderness she'd never seen in them before.

She felt a strange sense of unreality, as if she were in some kind of impossible dream. 'Where you belong...in my arms.' Had he really said that?

'You—you saw Crystal?' she forced out. She had to know what had happened.

'I did. And you'll never have to worry about her again, Taryn. I promise you. Neither of us will.'

Her throat went dry. 'Wh-what do you mean?'

'I mean that she's leaving Australia...on the first available flight to Spain. She's going to stay with her mother for a while...for quite a while.' His voice hardened as he ground out, 'She knows that if she comes back she's likely to be arrested and charged.'

'You—you mean she admitted—?'

'Not right away. But once I told her there was a witness, and that she was likely to be arrested, she crumpled. She begged me to save her...blaming *me* for driving her to such desperate lengths.' He drew in his lips. 'I'd made it clear to her last night that I wanted her out of my life...'

'Last night?' Taryn gulped. 'You told her last night?'

'I found her waiting for me when I got home. She'd found a door unlocked and had walked in. When I tried to get rid of her she burst into tears, claiming that she couldn't live without me, that she'd always loved me, that she'd do anything for me, live anywhere I wanted, even live with my father... Though she suggested,' he added with a curl of his lip, 'that he'd probably be safer and happier in a nursing home.'

Taryn raised shocked eyes to his. Poor Patrick, she thought. Crystal was a cruel, heartless bitch. Had Mike only just come to realise it?

'She begged me to give her another chance.' Mike gave a disgusted snort. 'She seemed to think...' his voice roughened '...that I'd turned to *you*, Taryn, as a substitute for *her*...that I'd only been attracted to you because you looked a bit like her.' He gave a brief, rasping laugh.

Taryn gulped, fingering her throat. Was he saying...he hadn't?

'I told her she was wasting her time, that I didn't love her and never would.' He paused, his voice gentling. 'I made it clear I was in love with *you*, Taryn...only you...and that I'd been attracted to you *despite* the fact that there were a few superficial similarities between you both, not *because* of them. I told her I'd learned from *her* to look beyond the surface dazzle, and that underneath there are no similarities whatsoever. Plain speaking is the only way to get through to Crystal.'

He tilted her face to his, gazing into her stunned eyes. 'It's true, Taryn... I love you.' His eyes swam over hers, brilliant aqua washing over dazed, luminous black. 'I love you more than I ever thought I was capable of loving anyone.'

Her breath caught in her throat, her eyes flaring in shocked wonder. Inside her heart was bursting with joy...with disbelief. 'There's something I want to tell you,' he'd said this morning. He'd wanted to tell her that there was nothing between him and Crystal...that *she* was the one he loved. Not that he and Crystal were getting back together...not any of the soul-destroying things she'd imagined!

Before she could find her voice Mike's lips were on hers, and she felt herself dissolving under their usual magic. A long moment later he drew back, to growl, 'I made it clear to Crystal that even if you wanted nothing to do with me—even if you were out of my life for ever—I would never want *her*.'

Her eyes clung to his. 'Mike, I—'

He pressed a finger to her lips. 'You don't have to say anything…' He moved his finger over her cheek, gently stroking, feeling the softness of her skin.

'What Crystal did today was pure spite…pure malice; there was no other reason for it.' Anger throbbed through his voice. 'She wanted to hit back at both of us. She was hoping the fire would destroy Fernlea…perhaps even destroy you too. Or at least drive you away…drive us apart.' She could feel his lips in her hair, brushing over its clean, silky softness. 'Who knows what goes through a malevolent mind like hers?'

She shivered. Crystal's reason for picking up her mare this morning was now chillingly clear. She'd wanted to make sure Glory was safely out of harm's way!

'I'm sure Crystal's regretting what she did now,' she ventured, realising that she felt more sorry for the girl than vengeful. If Crystal had truly, genuinely loved Mike, being cast aside last night could have temporarily unhinged her mind, driving her into an act of desperation that she might never normally have contemplated.

'Her only thought was for her own neck,' Mike rasped, but his eyes softened as they caught hers. 'She doesn't deserve your compassion, Taryn…a quality, by the way, that Crystal, sadly, has never possessed. As I realised very quickly.'

He had? She gulped. And yet he'd still gone on wanting her. Had it been a sort of love-hate thing? 'Would you really have her arrested if she came back?' The thought of having to see Crystal again…having to face her in court…and possibly speak up against her… She felt a shudder run through her.

Mike shook his head. 'That was simply a scare tactic.

I just wanted her out of our lives. Both of our lives. Now and for ever.'

'And you're not a vindictive person either,' Taryn said softly. 'Least of all towards someone you once loved.' She couldn't keep a faint wistfulness from her voice. Crystal's return must have tempted him, though, just a little...at least in the beginning. She'd tempted him once before, only she hadn't been a free woman then, so nothing had come of it. 'You—you must have been terribly hurt when she broke off your engagement...and then married someone else.'

His hands tightened round her arms, giving her a tiny shake. 'I was *relieved*, Taryn...not hurt. It was a great load off my mind when she married someone else.'

'A *load* off your mind?' She stared at him, her brow wrinkling.

He smoothed away her frown with tender lips. 'I was half afraid she might want me back after she'd cooled down...and force me to be more brutal the next time.'

Taryn snatched in her breath. 'Brutal? You...didn't *want* her back?'

'Hell, no. I'd woken up to her by then...to what a mean-minded bitch she really was, under that angel-faced charm. The scales fell from my eyes almost as soon as we announced our engagement. The way she treated my father was the last straw,' he rasped. 'She didn't want anything to do with him...or the dairy farm. She treated him like dirt.'

Sensing his hurt, his anger, Taryn reached up to stroke his rough cheek. She could understand now why Patrick had disliked Crystal so much...why he'd reacted so violently last summer when he'd thought Mike's ex-fiancée had come back into his son's life.

'I realised I'd made a ghastly mistake, but being the gentleman I am...' a sardonic half-smile curved his lips '...I gave her the chance to break it off first. Saving face…salvaging self-esteem…means a lot to women like Crystal.'

'How did you manage that?' she asked curiously, finding herself admiring him even more for considering the feelings of a woman he no longer even liked.

He shrugged. 'It didn't take much. When I wouldn't fall in with her plans for me—she wanted me to give up what I was doing to work for her father—and told her I'd be going away for several months to promote my injectable drench, she threw a tantrum like I've never seen. When that failed to move me she threw the ring back in my face…thinking *that* would bring me back into line. It didn't. I left that same day.'

Taryn swallowed…hard. So Mike had known all along what Crystal was like. And she'd thought his cold indifference was a cover for the hurt he still felt!

But… She bit her lip, her brow clouding.

'What's wrong?' Mike asked quickly. 'You don't believe me?'

'I… It's just…' She faltered. 'If you didn't care about her…' She paused, gulping. Suddenly the answer hit her. 'It's not true, is it…that you spent a night with Crystal last summer?'

Mike went still. 'A *night*? Where did you get an idea like that?' There was shock, anger, not guilt in his eyes. 'Did Crystal tell you that? And you *believed* her?'

She shook her head. 'Rory Silverman told me…the day you went off to America. He told me you'd met your ex-fiancée Crystal at that Rotary dinner you all went to, and that you'd spent the night with her.' She smiled ruefully up at him. 'You'd told me yourself that you intended to have a night of passion with an old flame, so I had no reason to doubt him.'

Mike swore. 'I just tossed that at you in the heat of the moment, out of pure jealousy. I've never looked at another woman since the day I met you.'

His fingers gripped her arms more tightly. 'Rory

Silverman's a lying swine.' If Rory had been there it might have been his neck Mike was gripping. 'I had a coldly polite two-minute conversation with Crystal that night, in a room full of people. She didn't like it when I told her I had to rush off. She said she hoped I wasn't rushing home to my next-door neighbour, because Rory Silverman was spending the night with you. And as she'd been sitting at Rory's table *I* had no reason to doubt *her*.'

Taryn groaned. '*That's* why you left for America without saying goodbye to me? Because you thought I was having an affair with Rory?'

'Well…you were, weren't you? You made no secret of it. Crystal just confirmed it.'

'Oh, Mike.' She shook her head, flushing in mortification. 'I let you think Rory had come back to my place that first night I met you because you were being so— so insufferably boorish. You *wanted* to think the worst of me. I've never encouraged Rory. Ever! He'd be the last man on earth I'd ever spend a night with. I never saw him on the night of the dinner. He only came to see me two days later to tell me about you and Crystal.'

'So…it was a case of the two of them injecting a little poison,' Mike ground out, 'to stop *us* getting together. And they almost succeeded.' He searched her face. 'That's why you've been so wary of me all this time…isn't it, my darling? You thought I still cared for Crystal?'

She snuggled her face deeper into his shoulder. *My darling…* The endearment sent a melting sweetness through her. 'And it's why you were so wary of *me*,' she whispered. 'And because I looked so much like Crystal…and came from a similar background.'

Mike tilted her face to his. 'I soon learnt how totally different you are. I can't believe now that I didn't see through Crystal from the start.'

'I can understand men finding her irresistible,' Taryn

said gently. 'She can be utterly captivating when she wants to be.' She could understand, too, how a man as stunningly good-looking and brilliantly clever as Mike must have been irresistible to Crystal.

His fingers closed round hers. '*You're* captivating without even trying,' he murmured, lifting her hand and pressing it to his lips. 'And it's genuine, not fake.'

She blushed. He seemed so sure…so sure of her. After his experience with Crystal, how could he *be* so sure?

He smiled as their eyes met, and she almost lost the thread of the conversation under the impact of the shimmering turquoise below the heavy brows. 'How you could ever have believed I would make comparisons…' He released her hand for a moment to trace her lips with a tender finger. '*Your* lips never curve in a mean, petulant pout or turn down in disdain or thin in contempt. *Your* voice never spits pure venom or whines or grates.'

He kissed her eyelids with a gentleness that melted her bones. '*Your* eyes never narrow in spite…or burn with hate.' He trailed his lips down her cheek, his breath heating her skin. As his mouth reached hers, something deep inside her contracted, bringing a piercing pleasure—and a fierce longing.

'You, my sweetest Taryn,' he murmured against her lips, 'are always caring and considerate, always thinking of others. I noticed that, right from the first day I met you, when you didn't want my father coming out in the storm. When you offered me a ride back from the forest. When you let me dry my clothes in your house. When you drove me home…'

She felt his fingers sliding through her hair, releasing it from the ponytail she'd retied earlier, letting the shiny black mass flow over his arm. 'You've been tying your hair back lately to avoid comparisons with Crystal, haven't you, you foolish girl? You're never to think like that again. I only see *you* when I look at you…however you wear your hair…however you dress…whatever lipstick you wear. Crystal's the last woman I'd ever compare you with.'

'Crystal married on the rebound, didn't she?' Taryn said gently. 'To show you she didn't care about your break-up. But she *did* care. And I can understand her wanting you back, Mike. What woman *wouldn't* want a gorgeous hunk like you? Not only a gorgeous hunk... you're a beautiful person through and through,' she said fervently, finding it hard to believe, even now, that he seemed to have chosen *her*.

'Are you saying...that *you* want me?' Mike asked guilelessly. 'Weren't you just being neighbourly today, when you risked your life to save me?'

She gave a soft gurgle of laughter. Suddenly the lamp-lit den seemed lighter, brighter, cosier. The gentle pitter-patter of rain on the roof was like music...a beguilingly romantic melody. 'I more than *want* you, Mike O'Malley,' she told him. 'I'm crazy about you. It's like a dream... I can't believe that you love *me*.' Only hours ago she'd thought she'd lost him...to Crystal.

He dipped his head and kissed her...his lips warm and very real on hers.

'Never doubt again, my darling. It's true...and always will be. And one day—you can have as long as you like—I hope that you'll do more than just want me...feel crazy about me. I hope you'll come to love me as much as I love you...and that you'll want to live with me for the rest of your life.'

Her lips parted. Didn't he *know*? Couldn't he tell?

'Oh, Mike,' she breathed. 'I do already. I *do* love you... I—I've known it for some time, but I thought—'

'You thought I might still feel something for Crystal.'

She nodded. She'd read all the signs wrongly... Crystal being at his house last night—the girl had made her presence known out of pure spite. The way Mike had kissed her so fiercely the night he'd left for the airport—he'd feared for her *safety*, knowing he'd be leaving her to Crystal's tender mercies for a week.

And he'd had reason to be afraid...

The fire...

She shivered. *A woman scorned, seeking revenge.*

'I love you, Mike,' she said, winding her arms round his neck, raking her fingers through the tumbled wildness of his hair. 'I'll always love you...and I can give you my answer right now. Nothing would make me happier than to live with you for the rest of my life.'

She flicked a look upwards in sudden apprehension. 'That's if...you *want* my answer now?' He'd rushed into a commitment once before...and lived to regret it.

'My foolish love, of course I do. I'm just amazed—overcome—that you feel the same way.' He gently rocked her in his arms. 'I've found my dream girl finally...and this time it's no illusion and I'm very, very sure.'

And then he made a confession that squeezed her heart.

'I knew, from the moment we met again after I came back from overseas, that the feelings I'd tried my best to squash from the day I first met you were the real thing all along... ' His eyes darkened with an emotion that shook her. 'And each day since I've been back I've come to love you more. The strength of my feelings scared me at first... I wasn't sure I could trust them.'

'Maybe just as well,' he'd said on the night the call from the hospital had interrupted their kiss. She smiled up at him, knowing now what he'd meant.

'It blows me away knowing you feel the same way...already.' Mike's lips nuzzled her throat. 'I thought you'd need more time...'

She shook her head, her eyes telling him just how certain she was.

'Mike...' She faltered. 'Remember how you asked me

once if I was selling Fernlea? If I *had* gone back to Melbourne to live, would you have bought it?'

He considered. 'I would certainly have put in an offer,' he admitted honestly. 'Moving into Fernlea would have saved me having to build a new house, as I've been intending to do...my father and I both being independent types who'd rather not live on top of each other.' His eyes held a glittering warmth. 'Dad would still have been within easy reach...only minutes away.'

'And with the two combined properties,' Taryn encouraged, 'you could have planted crops...expanded your interests... '

He frowned. 'What are you getting at, Taryn? You don't think I still—'

'But Mike, I hope you *do* still want to live at Fernlea!' she cried. 'That is...if you meant it when you said you wanted to live with *me* for the rest of your life.'

Understanding dawned in his eyes. 'Oh, I don't just want to *live* with you, my adorable Taryn... I want to *marry* you... I want you for my wife. But I'm not expecting you to give an—'

'But I *want* to give you an answer now,' she said with certainty. 'I *want* to be your wife...nothing could make me happier. And if your father wants to live with us, Mike, until he's back on his feet...'

Mike gave a soft chuckle, holding her gaze with his, his brilliant eyes blazing with his love for her. 'By the time we've arranged the wedding and walked down the aisle, my love, Dad will be well and truly back on his feet...back working on the farm...and he'll insist, if I know him, on staying in his own home, in his own bed. He's a tough, independent old codger.'

He was easing her off his lap as he spoke, drawing her to her feet. 'And he'll have the four of us living close by—Lucy and Smudge in the old house, and you and I at Fernlea—to make sure he's safe and well fed, with a spick-and-span house.'

'Of course we will,' she agreed with a warm smile. 'I'm going to like having Patrick for a father-in-law.'

Her mother might take a while to get used to the idea of her daughter marrying into the O'Malley family and living permanently in the Strzelecki Ranges of South Gippsland—she'd always hoped that her daughter would end up marrying a city businessman and giving up her horses and her unsociable country lifestyle—but underneath, Taryn suspected, she'd be more relieved than put out. Since the accident, her mother had despaired of her daughter ever marrying at all!

Mike's lips stopped her thoughts...stopping her heart at the same time. This was a different kiss from any other they'd shared...this time there were no doubts, no confusions, no reason to stop or break away. He paused only long enough to murmur against her lips, 'No more talking...just touching...feeling...revelling in our love for each other...'

And revel in each other they did...lips hungrily searching, eager hands roving, gasping breaths mingling with ecstatic moans as their senses soared to giddy heights, the blood in their veins heating, flaming out of control...until Mike eventually raised his head and drew back, glancing towards the door.

She asked in quick dismay, her voice a breathless squeak, 'You have to go already?'

He gave a soft chuckle, and caught her hands in his, crushing them to his chest. 'No, my darling, I don't have to go...' She heard the huskiness in his voice, felt the frantic beat of his heart. 'I was just thinking that you've never given me...a tour of your house.'

Her jaw dropped. He wanted a tour of the house *now*? Just when—

He laughed at the look on her face. 'I had in mind a tour of the bedrooms...of *your* bedroom in particular,' he murmured, and the relief in her eyes, the dawning smile on her lips and the glow reddening her cheeks made him laugh even more.

'Up the stairs,' she gulped out, her own voice as thick and hoarse as his, her body trembling in anticipation. 'Let me show you the way.'

'Verbal directions will do,' he suggested, sweeping her back into his strong, loving arms.

EPILOGUE

THE sky was clear and the autumn sun bright over the little country church in the Strzelecki Ranges not far from Fernlea. The rose-adorned pews were crammed with relatives, old friends, local friends, neighbours, old equestrian team-mates, vets, chemical engineers, close friends of her mother's and a few old mates of Patrick's...and there were more people gathered outside the church...interested spectators who'd just come to look.

The bride was late...but it wasn't Taryn who was holding up progress, it was Patrick, the man who'd proudly agreed to walk her down the aisle—once he'd recovered from his shock at being asked. He couldn't get his bow-tie to lie straight, and was refusing to budge until he did.

Taryn's mother was fluttering around, getting more flustered by the second at the delay. She still hadn't accepted Patrick in the role her daughter had chosen for him. In her eyes, it was flaunting tradition for the father of the bridegroom to give away the bride...it should, she'd argued, be a relative or close friend of the bride's family. But Taryn had held firm, insisting that nothing would make her happier than to have Patrick O'Malley hand her to his son on her wedding day.

'The photographer and the wedding cars are waiting,' her mother reminded them for the third time as Patrick continued to fuss and fiddle.

'I look ridiculous,' Patrick complained. 'I don't know why Mike had to insist on black tie.'

'Here, let me help,' Taryn soothed, handing her bou-

184

quet of cream roses to her bridesmaid, Hilary, an old equestrian friend, looking glamorous in an ankle-length gown of emerald-green silk.

Even though it wasn't a formal wedding by any means, Taryn knew why Mike had chosen black tie for himself, his father, and his best man. He'd wanted to do justice to *her*, knowing she was planning to wear traditional white with all the trimmings. Actually, her full-length gown wasn't white, but ivory…ivory lace, with a floating white veil and a headpiece encrusted with tiny pearls.

'Patrick, you look extremely handsome,' she assured him. 'I can see now where your son gets his good looks.' She brushed his hand away. 'Just stand still while I adjust it for you.' And she did, with no fuss whatsoever.

When they finally arrived at the church, there were gasps of admiration as the bride alighted from her highly polished vintage wedding car.

'She looks like a princess,' a young child piped up in a loud whisper.

'Isn't she beautiful?' gasped someone else.

'A dream.'

'Stunning!'

Taryn could feel the waves of warmth and goodwill sweeping over her as she mounted the steps of the church with Patrick beside her and Hilary leading the way. The warm welcome gave her confidence. Normally she no longer worried about her limp—barely even thought of it—but today was so special that she'd found herself wondering if it would be noticeable as she walked down the aisle. She wanted to be beautiful…perfect…for Mike.

But her worries slipped away as she stepped into the church on Patrick's arm and saw the friendly smiles…heard the excited buzz that rose above the sound of the Bridal March…felt the love pulsating around her…and met Mike's eyes as he turned his head to flash her a smile and drink in the sight of her.

Her limp didn't matter to Mike. It shouldn't matter to her. Her foot had improved anyway in the past three months, as it had regained more of its old strength and tone. Patrick never worried about his own slight hobble from his hip operation. He'd long since thrown away the stick he'd had to use for a time, and the crutches before that.

She gave Patrick's arm a squeeze. They could support each other down the aisle!

They did…with Hilary gliding ahead of them at the same serene, unhurried pace. When the bride eventually took up her position beside her future husband, Mike turned to smile into her eyes, and she smiled back, feeling his warmth and deep love flowing into her.

If Patrick was handsome in his hired dinner suit, Mike was breathtaking…a younger, more dynamic version of his father, with his father's brilliant eyes, his height, his powerful physique…and his mop of unruly hair—though Patrick's was pure white now, and he'd lost weight during his forced convalescence.

'Who gives this woman?'

'I do!' Patrick boomed, and there were chuckles from behind. Amused, affectionate chuckles rather than sniggers. Even Taryn's mother smiled.

They'd chosen a simple ceremony and it was soon over, with barely a dry eye in the church. Their kiss, in front of everyone, brought happy tears even to Grace Conway's eyes. Taryn's mother had met Mike before the wedding, of course—several times—and he'd won her heart as easily as he'd won her daughter's…not only her heart, but her approval too. She could see that her daughter was going to be in good, safe, loving hands. Perhaps it had helped that he was brilliantly clever and successful as well!

And her daughter's home in the Strzelecki Ranges wasn't really so far away, after all.

The wedding luncheon was held in Fernlea's tree-lined garden. Taryn had given in to her mother's wishes and allowed her to arrange the catering and the flowers, and a marquee in case of rain. But there was no hint of rain or clouds today, and the green lawns, lush after the recent rains, and the shady old English trees—with the grand old two-storey house overlooking both—made a perfect setting.

'Dreams do come true,' Taryn whispered to Mike as Smudge drove them to the airport later for a week's honeymoon in the Whitsunday Islands. 'Remember that day in the forest, Mike, when I opened my eyes and found you kissing me? I thought I was dreaming. I didn't see how any man in the real world could be so wildly good-looking. And now—I can hardly believe it—I'm married to my dream man.'

Mike lifted her hand and pressed his lips into her warm palm. 'And you, my lovely bride,' he murmured, 'are living proof that dream-*girls* exist too...that *my* dream-girl does, anyway. Our life is going to be one long dream come true.'

'We'll make sure of that,' she agreed, and raised her lips for his kiss.

Smudge, watching in the rear-view mirror, smiled.

JASMINE CRESSWELL

THE DAUGHTER

Maggie Slade's been on the run for seven years now.
Seven years of living without a life or a future because
she's a woman with a past. And then she meets Sean
McLeod. Maggie has two choices. She can either run,
or learn to trust again and prove her innocence.

"Romantic suspense at its finest."

—Affaire de Coeur

1-55166-425-9
**AVAILABLE IN PAPERBACK
FROM SEPTEMBER, 1998**

CHRISTIANE HEGGAN

SUSPICION

Kate Logan's gut instincts told her that neither of her clients was guilty of murder, and homicide detective Mitch Calhoon wanted to help her prove it. What neither suspected was how dangerous the truth would be.

"Christiane Heggan delivers a tale that will leave you breathless."

—Literary Times

1-55166-305-8
**AVAILABLE IN PAPERBACK
FROM SEPTEMBER, 1998**

DEBBIE MACOMBER

Married in Montana

Needing a safe place for her sons to grow up, Molly
Cogan decided it was time to return home.
Home to Sweetgrass Montana.
Home to her grandfather's ranch.

*"Debbie Macomber's name on a book is a guarantee
of delightful, warm-hearted romance."*
—Jayne Ann Krentz

1-55166-400-3
AVAILABLE IN PAPERBACK
FROM AUGUST, 1998